The Pot Thief
Who Studied
Pythagoras

The Pot Thief Who Studied Pythagoras

A Pot Thief Mystery

J. MICHAEL ORENDUFF

OPEN ROAD
INTEGRATED MEDIA
NEW YORK

Cover design by Kathleen Lynch

ISBN 978-1-4804-5878-9

This edition published in 2014 by Open Road Integrated Media, Inc.
345 Hudson Street
New York, NY 10014
www.openroadmedia.com

To my mother,
Billie Louise Grisham Orenduff (1914–2012),
who gave me a love of books,
and to my wife and lifelong gencon partner,
Lai-Kent Chew Orenduff.

The Pot Thief
Who Studied
Pythagoras

1

The two best things about being a shopkeeper are that your income isn't limited to some corporation's idea of what a salary should be, and you get to set your own hours.

The two worst things are that you don't have a salary to depend on every month, and . . . Well, it doesn't really matter what the other worst thing is if there's no money coming in.

Which was my situation in April. My shop is in Albuquerque's Old Town, and the last time any money had passed over the counter was during the Christmas rush. Which was actually more of a Christmas mosey since December had seen no more than a dozen shoppers and only one buyer. He carried away a beautiful antique Santa Clara pot that had been on my shelves for a dozen years, and I felt a twinge of regret when I handed it to him.

Of course my remorse was salved somewhat when I saw *Hubert Schuze* in the "pay to the order of" line of a fifteen-thousand-dollar check.

The fifteen thousand had paid the light bill and kept food on the table and champagne in the fridge, but it was now nothing more than a fond memory. So I was happy to see a potential customer lingering by my door.

At least I hoped he was a customer. The way he was looking furtively up and down the street, he might have been a hold-up man.

Or maybe he just didn't want to be seen entering a disreputable establishment.

Not that I think of my business that way. It's not an opium den or a Frederick's of Hollywood, but I do have a bit of a reputation in some circles.

He eventually worked up the courage to step inside, whereupon he removed his fedora, introduced himself as Carl Wilkes and gave me a card that read *New World Antiquities.*

"Sounds like an oxymoron," I commented.

He offered a half smile. I offered him a cup of coffee and a warning about my brewing skill. It had been steeping for hours, but he drank it unflinchingly. No milk, no sugar.

Wilkes wore a dull green flannel shirt buttoned all the way up to his neck and tucked into taupe gabardine trousers. The hat was moleskin. He was so thin and his clothes so neatly pressed that he could have been wearing the outfit during the pressing.

"If you're looking for old pots," I said to him, "you've come to the right place."

"Are you perhaps familiar with this one?"

I looked at the photograph he handed me. "Yes, I know it. A beautiful piece, a thousand years old and almost perfect except for a small chip in the rim. If you want to see it, it's on display at the Valle del Rio Museum at the University of New Mexico."

"I've already seen it," he said. "What I want to do is buy it."

"Well, you could make them an offer I suppose, but I don't think it's for sale."

He shook his head slowly. "I've tried that. Museums seldom sell things from their collections. But you're in the business of selling pots, so perhaps I can buy it from you."

"If I owned it," I assured him with a smile, "I would sell it to you gladly."

He looked straight into my eyes. "Perhaps you could acquire it."

I stared at him across the counter while I thought about that remark. Small arroyos laced his tan skin, and his thick beard was trimmed close to his face. The leathery skin pegged him around fifty, but perhaps he was only thirty and had spent too much time in the New Mexico sun. His dark, deep-set eyes gave him a shifty look until the warmth showed in his smile.

After thinking about it for a few moments, I gave the only response that came to me. "How?"

"I imagine there are ways," he said, "but that's not my concern." He glanced out into the street and then continued. "If I bought one of the pots in here today, I wouldn't ask how or where you got it. And if I were to come back in a few days and find a new pot in your shop, I wouldn't ask how or where you got that one either."

"Mr. Wilkes—"

"Call me Carl."

"Carl, are you trying to suborn a felony?"

The lines around his eyes lifted into another half smile. His eyes seemed liquid and lighter when he smiled. He said nothing.

"Suppose," I said, "I could somehow acquire the pot in question—legally of course—and offer it for sale. What price do you think it would fetch?"

"Twenty-five thousand dollars," he answered.

Now I was smiling, too.

In addition to selling traditional Native American pottery, I'm also a pot thief. I don't like the term, and I don't think it's a fair description, but that's what I am. At least that's what I've been since the 1980s when Congress passed the Archaeological Resources Protection Act extending the definition of thievery to cover buried pots on public lands. And who knows more about thievery than Congress?

Prior to that, it was legal to dig up old pots for fun and profit. Those of us who did the digging were called something a lot more exotic. We were known as "treasure hunters." It was an honest profession, even an honorable one. Most of what we know about the ancient civilizations of Mesopotamia, Egypt, Greece and Rome we owe to treasure hunters who unearthed their artifacts. If it were not for that most famous of treasure hunters, Howard Carter, Tut would still be under the desert sand, and his funereal loot would not be touring the world in all its splendor.

Selling old pots is quite lucrative providing you don't get caught digging them up, but that's only part of the appeal. The real reward is the thrill of the find, the sudden connection with the ancient past when you hold in your hands a pot that has lain unknown and untouched for a thousand years.

Carter said it best when, after years of searching, he got his first glimpse of Tutankhamen: "The youthful Pharaoh was before us at last. An obscure and ephemeral ruler had reentered the world of history."

Although I've never dug up anything as significant as an Egyptian pharaoh, I have brought some beautiful pottery back into the world of history and profited handsomely from doing so. But the pots I sell to wealthy collectors are excavated from the ground, not stolen from museums.

I don't apologize for digging them up. They belong to whoever finds them, and I refuse to let Congress make me out a thief. It's more than just being denied the fruit of my labor as a digger, more than merely losing the benefits of my talent for reading the land and knowing where to look for artifacts. Sure I like the money, and there's nothing else I want to do to earn a living. But what's just as important—maybe even more so—is the spiritual connection I feel with those ancient potters. It's like reaching back through time. When I finally feel the cool smooth clay beneath the sand, I'm touching the hand of the potter.

I know why she was there, because I found my way to that same sheltered dune using knowledge of the land she possessed a thousand years before I was born. I'm holding the pot she took with her to carry water or gather juniper berries. When I find that pot, I find her, someone like me who knew the feel of wet clay between her fingers.

Taking a pot from a museum wouldn't give me that same thrill. I knew that. Someone else had already experienced the moment of unearthing. The pot in the Valle del Rio Museum was no virgin.

So what if the thrill wouldn't be there. Twenty-five thousand dollars can be thrilling in its own way, especially since it was April and I had neglected to set aside from last year's adjusted gross income the thirty-one percent now due to the Internal Revenue Service.

I also owed a penalty because my quarterly estimated tax payments weren't large enough, which is a ridiculous rule because it's impossible to estimate my income. I admit it's petty, but I was feeling frustrated and maybe a little sorry for myself. The same government that wants to ban me from making a living also wanted me to know in advance that I'd have a fifteen-thousand-dollar sale at Christmas and send them the tax before I collected the money.

But there's no arguing with Uncle Sam. I owed the tax and I owed the penalty. The twenty-five thousand Wilkes was proffering would more than cover both.

When he asked me to think about it, I said I would. He told me he would be in the Hyatt for the next two days and invited me to visit him after I had thought it over. What he didn't know was I had already thought it over.

I wish I hadn't.

2

Thinking about the museum wasn't getting me anywhere. I even went so far as striking the pose—elbow resting on the knee, wrist curled back under the chin. But that made me think of Rodin, not pots.

So I gave up and walked down the street, across the plaza and over to Dos Hermanas Tortillería where my best friend Susannah and I can be found almost every evening unwinding from work with our mutual friend Margarita, the delightful daughter of Jose Cuervo.

Susannah's in her late twenties and unwinds easily from working the lunch shift at La Placita, which starts about ten in the morning for table set-up and menu review and ends about three when the dining room has been restored to some semblance of order. I'm forty-something and don't unwind as easily as I used to even though the only thing I was unwinding from was sitting behind the counter thinking about Wilkes and the museum.

We use the cocktail hour to talk about Susannah's bumpy road to love, her studies, my illegal treasure hunting and anything else that needs talking about. She was telling me about her day.

"Food coloring!" she almost shouted, her big eyes wide with disbelief. "Can you believe it?"

"Well," I replied, "you did say he was from Texas, and—"

"It was a rhetorical question, Hubert. And even Texans should know that blue corn tortillas come from blue corn. What kind of a restaurant uses food coloring anyway?"

I assumed that was another rhetorical question, so I just licked the last grains of salt off the rim of my glass and waved for a refill while Susannah continued to berate the customer who had asked her if blue corn tortillas had food coloring in them. I won't bother you with the whole story, but in the end he had cleaned his plate and she had put him in his place by pointing out that there was no blue residue anywhere to be found.

After she told me about the other interesting diners she had served that day, our second round arrived, and it was my turn. I told her about Wilkes' visit, and she asked if I intended to steal the pot.

"I'm not a thief."

"You steal pots."

"Well, technically. But that's just the government's view. In my mind, it's not stealing because the pots I dig up don't belong to anyone."

"Maybe the government's view is the one that counts. After all, they're the ones with the police."

"Good point," I conceded, "but there are few police wandering around the desert looking for treasure hunters. And even after you dig something up, who's going to call the police to report it?"

"Whereas a pot missing from the Museum would definitely be reported."

"Especially this one. It's one of only two intact Mogollon water jugs ever found."

"So that's why Wilkes is willing to pay twenty-five thousand for it?"

"Yeah, and it's obviously worth more than that. He probably has a collector he can sell it to, and I assume he plans a hefty markup."

She took a sip of her margarita and gave me her Mona Lisa smile. "I bet I know what you're thinking. You're thinking that if you had dug up that pot, it would be yours. So if you take it from the Museum, it will be like you dug it up and the Museum just served as the middleman. Am I right?"

She knows me better than I know myself.

"Something like that," I admitted. "I haven't thought it completely through. I do know this, though. If another pot hunter had found it, I certainly wouldn't entertain the idea of breaking into his house to steal it."

"Honor among thieves?"

I scowled. I think of myself as a decent person. If I see money fall from someone's pocket, I chase them down and return it. I've never seen a pot fall out of anyone's pocket, but if one did and I found it, I would return it. Of course, it would probably be just a handful of shards after the fall, but I wouldn't even steal another man's shards. But when I dig up a thousand-year-old pot, its rightful owner is long gone and obviously failed to bequeath it in his will. So I don't feel guilty about making it my own.

"Seriously," she continued, "I know you're a man of principle, but is a museum different from someone's house?"

"Maybe. It was the unholy trinity of professional archaeologists, museums and political correctness activists that got pot digging outlawed. And I'll tell you what I think of museums. They're places where—"

"Pots go to die," she said before I could.

"I guess I've told you that before?"

"Repeatedly."

"Well, it's true. What I object to is museums taking things out of circulation. Courtiers buried pharaohs with riches while the peasants lived like slaves. Today we put our valuables into museums instead of graves, but that helps the common man about as much as the gold in Tut's sarcophagus helped the Egyptian peasants. Buying and selling, goods changing hands, that's what makes an economy work."

"Spoken like a true shopkeeper."

"And proud of it. If Congress had given tax breaks to treasure hunters instead of criminalizing them, they could have added a few more percentage points to the gross national product, not to mention increasing what we know about the peoples of the past."

"That's why we have archaeologists."

"Right. Concentrating on one square meter on the edge of an artifact-rich site, their little brushes shifting a teaspoon of sand a day while some graduate student writes every move down in a spiral notebook."

I fumbled around for an analogy. "It's like the department of agriculture placing a fertile field off limits except to a handful of agronomists who are experimenting with micro lettuce while hungry people are barred from planting food crops."

"You're not exactly starving."

I shrugged. I felt better getting it off my chest. She caught the attention of our server, the lithesome Angie, and ordered a third round.

"Don't you have class tonight?"

Susannah is a perpetual part-time student at the University of New Mexico.

"It's a guest lecture on Frederic Remington. You can't face something like that on only two margaritas."

I drained my glass and asked why a psychology major would attend a lecture on Remington.

"Honestly, Hubie, sometimes I think you don't listen to me. I dropped psychology last semester. I'm majoring in art history now."

"Sorry. It slipped my mind, but now I remember."

Angie refilled our glasses, and Susannah asked her to bring more tortilla chips and salsa.

"The chips and salsa soak up the tequila. I'll be fine by seven."

"That's an interesting theory. Why did you choose art history?"

"The same reason I chose psychology—to meet guys. But all the guys you meet in psychology are psychotic. That's why they study psychology in the first place, to find out what's wrong with them. Did you know that?"

"Yes, I know that. In fact, I think I'm the one who told you that. Remember? When you told me you were going to switch to psychology? But you went ahead anyway, didn't you?"

"Geez, you sound like my mother."

"Sorry. I don't mean to be critical."

"Anyway, you're an artist. You should appreciate my new major."

"I'm not an artist. I'm a ceramicist. I make clay pots."

"That's art."

"Quick," I said, "name ten famous artists right off the top of your head."

"Let's see," she said and ticked them off on her fingers, "there's Michelangelo, Leonardo, Rembrandt, Vermeer, Van Gogh, Matisse, Gauguin, Picasso, Georgia O'Keeffe, and Andy Warhol."

"See? Not a potter in the bunch."

"Well, maybe you'll be the first one to become famous."

"I don't think so. Even if pots were art, I just make copies."

"But you do like art history."

"I do. And I admire you for exploring your intellectual horizons."

"I'm not exploring my intellectual horizons. I'm trying to meet a good man. To which I should say good luck or fat chance or something."

"Well, you're unlikely to meet one in art history. Most art historians are women, and the men—"

"I know. They're all gay."

"Well, maybe not all."

"The few I know are. And you're right—almost all art history students are women."

"If you knew that, why did you choose art history?"

"I know it *now*. I didn't know it then."

I leaned back in my chair and gave her an appraising look. "You know what I think? I think you did know it. I think you really are academically inclined, but you like to pretend you're in school just to meet men."

"Now you're going back to psychology. Let's order another margarita."

I looked down and discovered our glasses had emptied themselves while we were talking.

"If we have another one, how many will that be?"

"Four I think."

"Isn't that too many?"

"You know what you always say, Hubie—a bird can't fly on one wing."

"Neither can a bird fly on three wings."

"Exactly," she said. "A bird with three wings will be all lopsided and *really* unable to fly. At least four is an even number."

"I can't argue with that," I said—and I didn't.

3

The next morning I walked over to the University to visit the Valle del Rio Museum. I walked because I enjoy walking and because parking spots at the University of New Mexico campus are about as common as Nobel Laureates.

I didn't know whether I would eventually try to get the pot, but I figured it couldn't hurt to take a look around.

I was wrong.

It was a sunny spring day with a soaring New Mexico sky, the sun high over the peaks of the Sandia Mountains. Classes were in full swing and students scurried between buildings. No one paid any attention to me as I leaned against a tree and studied the windows and doors of the Museum.

Finally I went inside. I acted like a typical museum patron, staring at the works on display. Except that I wasn't looking at them. I was looking at walls, floors, ceilings, outlets, conduits, fixtures and everything else except the display pieces.

The Mogollon pot was in a side room, still displayed as I remembered it, on top of a plinth, a word even Ogden Nash couldn't rhyme. The velvet ropes stretched between four stanchions prevented curious patrons from touching the pot. There was no one else in the room. I gently lifted one of the stanchions and waited.

Nothing happened. No alarms sounded, no sirens wailed, no automatic doors slammed shut, no guards rushed in.

I removed the end of one rope from its stanchion and waited again. Same result. I placed the end of the rope quietly on the floor and stepped to the pot. Nothing happened. Evidently, there were no invisible laser beams. Nor any motion detectors. I listened for footsteps and heard none. The guards and the ticket takers were still in the front room.

I pulled two paper napkins from my pocket and, draping them over my hands, I lifted the pot up about an inch and carefully sat it back in precisely the same spot. Then I put the napkins in my pocket, stepped back outside the forbidden square and replaced the rope on the stanchion.

I now knew that I could get the pot off its pedestal with no problem. But what good was that knowledge to me? The windows were protected by steel bars. The front door was metal with a double-cylinder deadbolt lock. The basement had no entry from outside. It didn't even have window wells. There were no skylights. Patrons were required to check all parcels, book bags, purses and briefcases at the front desk before passing through a metal detector, which was the only way in or out. Exiting with any sort of package would be impossible unless the entire staff were chloroformed.

And even that wouldn't work because the only security camera I could see was aimed at the front door. The pot was about eighteen inches tall and perhaps fourteen across, so I couldn't smuggle it out in my pockets unless I broke it into shards. Which would lower its value considerably below twenty-five thousand, not to mention make a lot of noise and attract the guards.

There was no way for me to get into the building when it was locked at night. There was no way to sneak anything out when it was open during the day. I was stumped.

But when I was a math student, many of the theorems I was assigned seemed at first glance to be unprovable. I discovered you have to ignore first impressions and keep thinking about it, looking at it from different angles and asking questions that might lead to a new perspective. Quixotic questions like how could you show the theorem *can't* be proved? Or what would have to be the case if you *were* to prove it? Or how would you change the theorem to make it *easier* to prove? These seemingly paradoxical questions—which in my mind always contained *italicized words*—often led me to see a path to the solution that I hadn't seen by taking the normal and straightforward approach. So rather than conclude that getting the pot out of the Museum was impossible, I decide to seek an ingenious and creative solution.

It took me forty minutes to walk back to my shop. I used the time to let my creative juices flow. Evidently, the flow was more of a trickle. When I got back to my shop, I still had no clue how to get the pot out of the Museum.

4

I once had a bell mounted on a little arm above the front door of my shop. It tinkled—rather merrily I thought—whenever a visitor crossed my threshold.

My nephew, Tristan, determined to bring me into the electronic age, replaced my bell with a contraption that shines a laser beam across the door and bongs when it's interrupted. The beam, not the door. The door is made of three-hundred-year-old piñon and couldn't be interrupted by anything measuring less than 7.5 on the Richter scale.

Shortly after I arrived back at the shop and opened for business, the bong let me know the beam had been interrupted. The interrupter wore a size fifty windowpane suit with panes that were too large and lapels that were too small. He had a pasty complexion and razor-cut hair held in place by either the world's strongest hair spray or shellac. The desert wind had started early, and the morning's clear sky was now fuscous with blowing sand. Despite the wind, not a single strand of my visitor's pale brown hair was out of place. He looked at me and then he looked around the store like he intended to purchase the place.

The suit, haircut and demeanor said federal agent. Maybe Tristan was right to install the laser. A tinkling bell doesn't put you on alert like a grating bong.

Razor-cut reached the counter, produced a leather folder, flipped it open to reveal a badge and then quickly flipped it shut. At least I assumed it was a badge. It could have been a turquoise-and-silver squash blossom for all the look I got at it.

"Agent Guvelly, Bureau of Land Management. You Hubert Schuze?"

"Happily so."

"We're investigating the disappearance of a Mogollon pot."

I stood there stunned. I haven't stolen it yet, I thought. I haven't even *decided* to steal it. I don't know *how* to steal it. How could he be investigating a theft that I haven't even attempted?

"We have reason to believe you may know something about it."

I just stared at him. This can't be happening, I thought. Then it came to me. I had been spotted at the Museum. Someone had stolen the pot after I left, and they thought I did it. But I still couldn't think of anything to say, much less how someone could have done the impossible and transported the pot out of the Museum.

"Well?" he asked.

I noticed his lips didn't move when he spoke.

"Well what?" I asked stupidly.

"Do you know anything about it?"

"I know it was still there when I left," I said with a quaver I couldn't suppress.

He gave me a quizzical look. At least I thought it was quizzical. With his broad face and frozen countenance, it was hard to judge what sort of look he had.

"When was that?" he asked.

"When was what?" Stupidity seemed to be working, so I decided to stick with it for now.

"When was it that you last saw it?"

"This morning."

"So you admit it," he said. "Where is it?"

Admit what? I thought. "It was in the Museum where it's been ever since I can remember."

"The Museum?"

"Yes, the Museum."

"What museum?"

I was tempted to ask "Who's on first?" but this didn't seem the time for levity. So I said, "The Valle del Rio Museum at the University."

"Don't play games with me, Schuze."

I tried to affect a smile both humorous and innocent, but probably got banal instead. "I'm confused. What exactly are you asking me about?"

He moved uncomfortably close to me. "I'm asking about a Mogollon water jug that was stolen from park headquarters in Bandelier."

So that was it. He was talking about the *other* Mogollon water jug.

Guvelly continued, "Our files say you've been stealing pots from federal land and selling them for many years."

"Sometimes asserted—never proved."

"All that means is you haven't been caught yet."

"A less cynical person might say it proves I'm innocent. Isn't there something in the constitution about that?"

"You're a wise-ass, Schuze. But I don't care about that because I'm going to nail you on this one."

I have already admitted to you that I unearth pots from the soil entrusted to the BLM and sell them to discerning collectors. But I had never at that point stolen anything from inside a building, and the idea of being "nailed" for something I hadn't done seemed at once grossly unfair and alarmingly possible.

"Look," I said earnestly, "I don't know what you're talking about. I've been to Bandelier many times, but only as a tourist. I don't know anything about a missing pot from there."

"Okay, play dumb. You already know, but I'll tell you anyway. It's a large water jug thought to be from the Mogollon. But you won't be able to sell this one. It's unique, it's important and it's catalogued. If it shows up anywhere on the face of the earth, we'll find it and trace it back to you. So play it smart this time and turn it over. If you voluntarily return the pot, maybe we can cut you some slack."

He wrote something on a card and handed it to me. "Think it over and call me. I'm at the Hyatt."

He opened the door, and I watched him and his hair move unperturbed into the wind.

I knew the pot he was talking about. The Mogollon lived in what is now southeastern New Mexico until a thousand years ago when they mysteriously disappeared. They were one of the three ancient peoples of the region, the other two being the Hohokam and the Anasazi. Except for archaeologists and a few treasure hunters, no one is aware the Hohokam or the Mogollon ever lived. The Anasazi, on the other hand, have somehow achieved celebrity status. If the map of prehistoric Native Americans were on the cover of *The New Yorker*, the Anasazi would be in Manhattan and the Mogollon in New Jersey.

First Wilkes asks me to steal the Mogollon water jug from the University. Then Guvelly informs me that the only other extant Mogollon water jug is missing from Bandelier. You can probably figure out what my first thought was. Right—that Wilkes stole the Bandelier jug for his client. But why would Guvelly think I stole it? It's true I was expelled from graduate school for selling pots I found during a summer dig, but that was before it was illegal.

I think the real reason the University kicked me out was because I showed up the faculty team by finding three beautiful specimens all by myself, away from the official site they had selected based on their archaeological expertise, a site that turned out to be a dry hole.

Being booted from college would hardly be a matter of federal concern, and I've never been arrested. At least I hadn't been at that point. I would be a few days later, but not for theft. I had a clean record when Guvelly came calling, and I just couldn't figure out why he would think I stole a pot from Bandelier.

Nor could I figure out if I should be worried about Guvelly and Wilkes both being at the Hyatt.

5

I walked over to Dos Hermanas feeling sheepish about having visited the Museum, so I didn't say anything about it at first because I knew Susannah would taunt me about being a burglar.

"I was visited by a pot cop," I said instead, picking up the drink she had ordered for me.

As I took my first sip, she replied, "Have you been growing marijuana?"

"Not that sort of pot—clay pots, the kind I sell in my shop."

She raised her eyebrows. "They have police for those?"

"I'm afraid so. Agents of the Bureau of Land Management whose job is to enforce things like NAGPRA."

"Sounds like a pill for men who can't—"

"It's a law, Susannah. The acronym stands for Native American Graves Protection and Repatriation Act. There's another one called ARPA, the Archaeological Resources Protection Act. They try to keep people from taking artifacts created by Native Americans."

"Why bother? Indians sell their stuff right here in Old Town every day."

"Not those Indians. Ancient peoples who lived in this area thousands of years ago."

"That's the stuff you steal, right?"

"You know I don't think of it as stealing because the things I dig up don't belong to anyone. But the pot Guvelly was interested in wasn't dug up, at least not recently. It was stolen from a display case in the park headquarters building at Bandelier."

"But it was dug up at some point, right? And some people think all those pots, including the ones already dug up, belong to today's Indians."

"Some people do think that, but their opinion is ridiculous," I said, waving their opinion away symbolically with the hand that wasn't grasping my margarita. "A thousand years from now some anthropologist will dig up our nonstick pans and treat them as ancient artifacts. Most of what they surmise about the people who made them will be wrong. They'll say the coated pans were used only for ceremonial occasions and their manufacture is a lost art when in fact we will probably discover the coating causes cancer or hives or something and just stop making them."

I have formulated over the years a set of anthropological theses I call Schuze's Anthropological Premises. I abbreviate them SAP, which is what some people think I am for believing them. But I think they are insightful. SAP number two says that evolution is not over. The first humans were short little hairy creatures who ate raw meat and shat on the ground. But they could talk and that makes them humans. It took about a million-and-a-half years for those first hunter-gatherers to evolve into modern humans who now eat raw fish and use toilets, and you can call that progress if you want to.

The Mogollon didn't make the evolutionary cut, and we have no idea whether they have any descendants. In fact, the concept of a Mogollon people is a white anthropologist's creation based on a few artifacts. For all we know, there may have been a number of people in that area who were ethnically distinct.

I never dig on reservations. God knows we left the native peoples small enough territories. The least we can do is respect what little land they still have. But artifacts with no direct connection to today's Indians belong to whoever digs them up, and I explained that to Susannah.

"I think of my trade as harvesting the riches of the earth, sort of like mining. Anyone resourceful enough to dig up trinkets ought to be able to keep them."

"Trinkets?" She gave me her mischievous smile. "What about someone resourceful enough to steal them out of a display case at Bandelier?"

"I think we just established that I mine the earth for its riches. I don't break into buildings and steal things. I'm not a burglar."

She ran her finger around the saltless rim of her glass and gave me another mischievous smile. "You will be if you do what Wilkes wants you to do."

"Maybe," I muttered.

Susannah asked me to tell her what Guvelly had said, so I recounted the entire conversation.

"Play it smart? Nail you? He actually talked like that?"

"Probably calls himself a G-man, too," I said.

"How did he look when he said it?"

"He stared right at me. His eyes never moved."

"You said his lips didn't move either."

"That's right."

"And his skin was chalky white?"

"I believe I said 'pasty,' but right again."

"That's creepy. Maybe he was from a wax museum."

I pictured Guvelly in wax. It wasn't hard to do. Then I asked Susannah about the lecture on Remington.

"It was awful. Guns, spurs, horses, ropes—not a single thing a girl would like."

"Most girls like horses."

"Not these horses. They had flared nostrils and wild eyes."

"I don't think Remington did any My Little Pony paintings."

"If he had, he would probably have cast them being spooked by a rattlesnake. He's like the official artist for Marlboro."

My glass had salt around its rim. Hers did not. Other than that one difference, we agree on all others aspects of the perfect margarita—never from a mix, always with silver tequila, never frothed or frozen, and never with strawberries, raspberries, peach liqueur, peppermint swizzle sticks, crumbled Hershey bars or any of the other countless adulterations which the noble *Nuestra Señora de Agave* has suffered in recent years.

Tequila is now one of the most popular distilled spirits in the United States, but I wonder why people in Boston or Birmingham like it. Its prime appeal to me is that it tastes like the desert—saline, organic and slightly viscous like the juice of the cactus it's distilled from.

I don't understand why anyone would drink *añejo*, the aged tequila whose amber color comes from being aged in wood casks like scotch or bourbon. If you want woody liquor, order those two. Don't adulterate good tequila. Pour it in a shot glass and hold it up to the light. Try to discern the ever so slight tincture of green. Hold it on your tongue and feel its volatile vapors chase the fog from your sinuses. Then let it roll down your throat like warm silver.

Why do I drink it in margaritas? Because pure shots send me straight to Margaritaville.

The agave is Mexico's national treasure, their answer to Canada's maple trees or our waves of amber grain. Mexican art is replete with images of the agave, a source of native pride, something not brought by the conquistadores. And New Mexico is part and parcel of Old Mexico, a stretch of the high Sonoran Desert stolen by the USA.

"You're not giving up on art history, are you, Suze?"

"No, you've got to take the bad along with the good."

"And what is the good?" I inquired.

"You sound like Socrates. I think he said the good is one of the Forms."

"Is philosophy another of your former majors?"

She shook her head. "I took it for general education. It was supposed to be an introduction to philosophy, and I was excited. I thought we'd be discussing how the universe began and what happens when you die. But all the instructor ever talked about was Socrates living in a cave."

"I think that was an allegory."

"No, I'm pretty sure it was a cave. There were prisoners chained to a wall and people crossed in front of them with cut-out figures of animals and houses and stuff, and a fire from behind threw shadows on the cave wall. The prisoners thought the shadows were real animal shapes because that's all they had ever seen. Or maybe they thought the shadows were real animals. I'm not too clear on that part. But the idea was that the prisoners are like us. We think what we see is real, but . . . Oh, I get it—allegory. I wasn't paying attention. You don't think I'm stupid, do you? I mean 'allegory' isn't a word you hear every day, and when you said it—"

"I know you're not stupid, but I may be." It was time to own up to sort of planning a theft from the Valle del Rio Museum. "Guess what I did today."

She gasped. "You stole that pot from the Museum?"

"No, but I did go there to look around."

She laughed and said, "You cased the joint!"

"I guess you could call it that," I admitted. "That's why Guvelly's visit unnerved me. I went to the Museum and looked at the pot just to see if I might be able to do it. I even picked it up. But I left it right where I found it and went home. Then right after I got home, he showed up and said they were investigating the theft of a Mogollon pot."

"And you thought he meant the one you had just looked at."

"Exactly. It was like an episode from Twilight Zone."

"I love that show."

"Yeah, I used to enjoy it, too. But this wasn't like watching it. It was like being *in* it. I felt like I'd been under surveillance, and the people watching knew I'd gone to the Museum. But they didn't just know what I did. They knew what I was *thinking*. I thought he was going to arrest me."

"What could he arrest you for? You hadn't done anything."

"I had committed larceny in my heart."

"Who said that? Wait, I know. It was Jimmy Carter. Except it wasn't larceny. It was lust."

"Lust is better," I said, "and also not illegal."

"Neither is stealing if all you do is think about it."

"I'm not so sure. I think planning to commit a burglary is a felony even if you don't actually go through with it."

"Hey, you're right. I remember Bernie Rhodenbarr mentioning that you can be arrested just for having burgling tools on you even if you don't use them."

I stared at her blankly. "Who is Bernie Rhodenbarr?"

"He's the burglar in those books I told you about."

"Oh, right," I said. Susannah has the endearing habit of talking about fictional characters as if they lived down the street from her.

"You didn't have any burglar tools on you, did you?"

"I had a couple of napkins that I used to lift the pot."

The way Susannah holds her wide shoulders back could almost seem military except she looks so relaxed and natural doing it. But when she's perplexed, she does this thing where she lets her shoulders fall forward and her long neck tilt back. She was doing that now and staring at me. "You didn't want to leave fingerprints?"

"No, I didn't want to damage the pot. Oil from your hands can stain pottery."

"That was considerate of you. So you didn't use the napkins as burglar tools. And anyway, I don't think napkins would count no matter how you used them."

"It doesn't matter if I had burgling tools. I was there trying to figure out how to steal the pot. That has to be as much intent as merely carrying around a crowbar."

"But they didn't *know* you were planning to steal it."

"I know that. But when Guvelly showed up like he had trailed me from the Museum and asked me about the pot, I couldn't think straight. It was like when you were a kid thinking about some mischief, and then you see your mother looking at you. You're positive she knows what you're thinking."

"That's just guilty conscience."

I knew she was right, but it still felt strange. I couldn't escape the feeling I had barely averted a disaster, even though that wasn't true. Guvelly didn't even know I had been at the Museum until I told him. No one was watching. I had nothing to worry about. Right?

Susannah canted her head and said, "Tell me honestly. When you had that pot in your hands, did you think for just a moment about walking out with it?"

"I thought about how much I would like to have it. It's an amazing piece of work, and it's survived over a thousand years with just a little chip out of the rim. But I didn't think about carrying it out."

"Why not?"

"The building is too secure. The windows have steel bars. The door has a double-cylinder deadbolt. The front has a security camera. There are at least two guards plus other employees around. There's no way to get that pot out."

"So you won't be able to collect the twenty-five thousand."

"I'm afraid not. I guess I'll just have to earn my tax money legally."

I was trying to get Angie's attention, but Susannah said, "One's my limit. I have a date tonight."

"Someone new?"

"Of course someone new. You wouldn't expect me to go out again with any of the losers I've dated in the past, would you?"

"So who is the latest contender?"

"He is soooo handsome. He has that LA look—spiky gelled hair, olive skin, and shoulders—"

"You'd like to rest your head on."

"Well, for starters maybe. He smells good, too. Not a cologne smell. I can't describe it, but it's tantalizing. He must be giving off profiteroles."

"I think maybe you mean pheromones. Is he a student?"

"No, he was the guest lecturer on Remington. He's actually from LA Can you imagine that? Me, a simple ranching girl, going out with someone from LA?"

"He's the lucky one. How much better a ranch girl than one of the phonies in Southern California."

I enjoy our conversations for what she says, but I like the way she says it almost as much. She is free from both that irritating nasal whine many young people have today and their affectation of ending every sentence with a tonal upswing.

"He's just staying through the weekend," she said. "I got to be part of the small group that showed him through the Museum after his talk—a private tour—and he asked me out. He wanted to go out right then, but I'd already had all those margaritas, and I didn't feel like I could be very charming. Plus, what would I do if he wanted to buy me a drink?"

I looked at her blankly. "I give up. What would you do?"

"That's the problem. There's nothing you can do. If you say no, then he won't have one, and right away you're off to a bad start because most dates start with a little getting-to-know-you over drinks. Also, if I refused a drink he might think I don't drink, and who wants to date someone who doesn't drink?"

"Who indeed?"

"But if I *did* let him buy me a drink, it would have been my fifth one, and I might have started acting silly. So I suggested tonight would be better."

Although she didn't have another drink, I did. I took a sip when it arrived to make sure it was as good as the first one. It was. Then I looked up and the mysterious Angie was still standing there, her dark eyes looking at me from under those long lashes.

"Mr. Schuze?"

"Yes, Angie."

"I need to tell you something. I'm not supposed to say anything, but I have to because you are . . . Well, it just seems wrong not to tell you even though he made me promise I wouldn't."

I gave her an avuncular smile. "Who are you talking about?"

"He's a federal agent, and he was asking questions about you."

"Yes, I know about him. He thinks I did something wrong, but I didn't. I'm not worried about it. I won't let anyone know you told me about him."

"So you're okay?"

"I'm okay."

She started to walk away. "Angie," I said, and she turned and looked at me. "Thanks for telling me."

Her wide smile softened her angular face. "We can't afford to lose our best customer." She swirled gracefully away, her long tiered skirt rustling like banana leaves.

The wind had died down as it almost always does at night, and I sat easily in the dry brisk evening enjoying the margarita and the scents of Dos Hermanas—the *masa* from the enchiladas, the smoke from the piñon logs in the fireplace and Angie's lemony perfume.

6

The only place I like better than Dos Hermanas is my own house.

I own, in partnership with the Old Town Savings Bank, the east third of a north-facing adobe located half a block off the plaza. The house was built in 1685, although it's impossible to know which parts are original and which parts belong to the countless remodels that have taken place over the last three centuries. There are four entrances—the front one to the shop, a back door out the kitchen that opens onto an alley and two doors on the east side that open off the bedroom and living room respectively into a small patio. Come to think of it, I don't know if the two doors to the patio can properly be called entrances since the area is entirely surrounded by an eight-foot adobe wall, so that entering from the east would require a big leap or a tall ladder.

Before I bought the place, it was a kitsch palace selling beaded purses from Malaysia, cactus candy from Canada, feathered head-dresses from Honduras and soft-serve ice cream from a chemical plant in the suburbs of Denver. Actually, I'm not certain where the chemical plant was. I'm pretty sure nothing in the shop was made in New Mexico.

When I was dismissed from the University, I sold the pots that led to that event and used the money for a down payment on my part of the building. Being kicked out of college didn't bode well for a job search, so I decided to start my own business.

Since dismissal also meant loss of my student housing, I needed a place to live. That was before the current trend of college graduates moving back in with their parents, so I never considered that an option.

The back portion of the space had been the storeroom, its walls a combination of exposed adobe, cement plaster, dirt plaster, plywood and the odd cardboard patch here and there. I hired day laborers to strip everything down to the bare adobe.

I'm a potter, so I know clay. Some generous friends call me an artist, but I am an artisan at best. Making pottery is no more a fine art than is trimming trees into topiary.

When all the walls of my residence had been repaired, I set about plastering them with traditional adobe plaster. The formula calls for clay, sand, water, finely chopped straw, prickly pear cactus juice and donkey manure. Put in a blender and serve it over ice at Dos Hermanas and they might call it a *cóctel de caliche*. It couldn't taste any worse than Campari.

I left out the prickly pear juice and the donkey manure, but mixed in everything else including the straw, which makes unfinished adobe glisten in the sunlight and made the conquistadores think they had discovered the Seven Cities of Gold. They must have been having a few cocktails themselves.

The final result was spectacular. The plaster follows whatever irregular shapes existed in the walls and ceilings. The final coat is a brilliant white with the geometry of a Georgia O'Keeffe painting. I had intended to hang a few prints, but the flow of the surfaces is so soothing that I can't bring myself to disrupt it. So the walls remain bare, a sort of art form themselves.

The floor of my living quarters is piñon pine sanded to its natural color and waxed. Because the boards are neither stained, lacquered, nor coated with polyurethane, they emit on hot days the sweet scent of piñon, carnauba and beeswax. I walked over that floor from living quarter to workshop to shop and opened the door for business.

Standing in front of it was Emilio Sanchez. He removed his hat and said, *"Buenos días, Señor Uberto."*

"Buenos días, amigo. Ha subido temprano."

The sun had not yet peeked over the Sandia Mountains to the east and the air was crisp and still. Emilio wore work boots, khaki pants, a chambray shirt and a denim jacket. The pants and shirt were freshly washed and pressed, but the boots were scuffed and the hat was sweat-stained.

"It is not so early. When you are an old one like me, you do not sleep so well."

I invited him in, shut the door and left the Closed sign facing the street.

"You must not close your shop because of me," he said.

"Don't worry. There won't be any customers this morning."

We went to my kitchen table where I gave him a cup of coffee and an apology for it in advance. Emilio carries himself like an eighteenth-century duelist, erect and proud. Sixty years of manual labor have scarred his hands and darkened his skin, but both his posture and his spirit remain unbowed.

He sat upright in his chair, nodded to me and took a sip. He placed the cup on the table and crossed his hands in his lap. "Uberto, I have brought from the doctor a paper I do not understand. My English is not so good."

"Your English is excellent. Not even an English teacher can decipher medical papers."

"What means *decipher*?"

"It is almost the same word in Spanish, *decifre*."

"Ah. The same word but sound different."

I read the paper. It was an explanation of the requirements for a patient undergoing dialysis. After I explained it to him, I asked if he had another paper from the doctor.

"Yes, I have this other paper you speak of, but I am ashamed to—"

"Señor Sanchez," I said, "you must not prevent me from following the wishes of my parents. Give me the bill so that I can arrange for the insurance to pay it."

"But I worry that you—"

"You worry about Consuela. I'll worry about the bills."

Consuela Saenz—she didn't become Consuela Sanchez until I was in college—was housekeeper to my parents, second mother to me and cook to all three of us. I have three skills—making pots, speaking Spanish, and cooking Mexican food—and she taught me two of them.

"I do worry about her," Emilio said. "It is a bad sickness."

"It is," I agreed, "but people live for many years with this condition."

"This is also as the doctor says. He tells Consuela she can live to one hundred."

"And what does she say?"

He looked up toward the ceiling. "She say she does not want to be one hundred. She just want to live long enough to see a grand-child."

"That sounds like her."

"She also tell me, Uberto, that she gives thanks to the Virgin every day for your parents."

"She was very good to them. And to me. Of course she spoiled me. I am never satisfied with Mexican food unless she has cooked it."

It was good to see him smile. "Then I hope you will enjoy this small gift," he said and removed a sack of breakfast burritos from his pocket.

7

As I predicted, no customers came in that morning.

Which was a mixed blessing. On the one hand, I could have used a good sale. On the other, it gave me time to eat the entire sack of breakfast burritos, a quantity so large it took half a bottle of New Mexico's finest champagne to wash them down properly. And if you're surprised by the phrase "New Mexico's finest champagne," you haven't tasted Gruet.

After breakfast, I pulled out an anthology of articles about Pythagoras and started reading them. I think most bestsellers are inane. Why would anyone want to read books with titles like *The South Beach Diet*, *Reinventing the Family*, or *Investing in Globalization*? But I admit that an anthology on Pythagoras is arcane even by my standards. I had checked it out of the library only because I commented on a poster of Pythagoras near the reference librarian's station, and she said there was a new collection of articles about him that were interesting. The next thing I knew she had placed the volume in my hand, and I took it so as not to disappoint her.

I started college as a math student, but all I knew about Pythagoras was what everyone else knows—he discovered the theorem that has been the curse of a hundred generations of eighth graders. The Pythagorean Theorem tells us that the square of the two short sides of a right triangle is always equal to the square of the hypotenuse, a piece of information most people forget the morning after their geometry class ends.

What I didn't know is that Pythagoras was also a world traveler, philosopher, mystic and poet. The frontispiece of the volume had this poem attributed to him:

Speak not nor act before thou hast reflected, and be just.
Remember we are ordained to die,
That riches and honors easily acquired are easy thus to lose.
As to the evils which Destiny involves,
Judge them what they are, endure them all and strive,
As much as thou art able, to deflect them with good.

I thought Pythagoras expressed some noble ideals, and had it been New Year's Eve, I might have adopted a resolution to follow them, especially since "riches easily acquired" could describe digging up pots.

I had thought poetry without rhyme was a recent aberration, but I guess it's been around for over two thousand years. Or maybe it rhymes in Greek. With or without rhymes, I suspect his poetry would appeal to more people than his theorem, and it has the added advantage that so far as I was able to determine, none of his poems include the word "hypotenuse," which would be almost as difficult to rhyme as "plinth."

I became so absorbed in Pythagoras that I didn't see the young lady until the bong signaled her entrance. She had a wide face with good cheekbones and a slightly misaligned nose. She was about five foot three inches tall with a full figure and more hip than is considered desirable these days but would have made Renoir jump for his canvas and brushes.

Her jeans were dirty and her hair disheveled. She stopped a few paces inside the door and gave me the sort of smile that indicated she was seeking approval to enter. The smile was on full lips. The smear of lipstick matched the heavy makeup.

"Come in," I said, trying to reassure her. She smiled again and glanced around the shop.

"How much do these pots cost?"

"All different prices. Do you see one you like?"

She scanned the room. Then she approached a shelf.

"That one's pretty," she said, pointing to a San Ildefonso *olla* done by Martina Vigil around 1900.

"That's one of my favorites," I said

She picked it up and my heart stopped beating. I walked to her casually so as not to provoke any sudden movement and gently took the pot from her hands. I didn't want to scold her, so I held it up and pointed out a few of its design features.

Then I put it back on the shelf and told her it was fifty thousand dollars.

"Wow! I guess I'll have to buy two of them," she said.

Standing close to her, I could tell she was younger than I had thought, college-age maybe, except she didn't look like a college student. I recognized the aroma of the cheap perfume samplers from a gift shop down the street and, underneath that, another faint scent that hinted at the need for a shower. Part of her full bottom lip was swollen.

"I'm Kaylee," she said.

"Hi, Kaylee. I'm Mr. Schuze."

"Wow, what a cute name. Do you have a first name?"

"Hubert," I answered.

She smiled again. "Do you, like, have anything to drink?"

"I have water and coffee—but it's not very good."

"What about something stronger."

I raised my eyebrows. "You mean alcohol?"

"Sure. You have any vodka?"

"No, I don't. Are you old enough to drink?"

She put her hands on her hips and pushed them out to one side. "I'm old enough to know better, too."

"Well, you could have fooled me." I hesitated for a moment and then said, "Listen, I have some work to do in the storeroom, and I need to close up the store while I do it. So thanks for coming in to see the pots, but I—"

"I could watch it for you," she said.

"Huh?"

"I could watch the store while you worked in the storeroom."

"Um, it's nice of you to offer, but I'm particular about my pots. Well, you already know how expensive they are, right? So I don't like to keep the store open when I can't be here to personally keep an eye on them."

"You wouldn't have to pay me. I could be like a temporary sales-girl that you didn't have to pay."

I shook my head. "No, sorry."

She stared at me for a moment. "You want me to leave now?"

"I do. I really need to close up now."

"Okay, that's cool. Thanks for letting me look at the pots, Hubert."

She was almost to the door when I said, "Kaylee," and she turned around. "Are you okay?"

"Sure," she said and then just stood there. After a few seconds she pulled the door open and left. The wind had kicked up, and I watched her walk toward the plaza with her hair fluttering behind.

I rotated the sign to *Closed* and was about to lock the door when Guvelly turned the corner and spotted me. If only Kaylee hadn't lingered at the door, I could have made a clean getaway.

He asked if I had thought about what he said to me yesterday. His lips were still rigid, and I noticed they were mismatched, the bottom one being wider. Without his upper lip being stretched, his mouth would have no corners.

I said, "I think you summed up the situation when you said I couldn't sell such a recognizable pot. So why would I steal it?"

"Maybe you just wanted to add it to your collection."

"You're welcome to look around. I won't even insist on a warrant."

He glanced around the shop as if he might take me up on the offer. Then he said, "I don't expect you to have it here. But if you do have it and are willing to return it, something might be worked out."

I was curious where he was going with this. "What sort of something?"

"You might claim you didn't steal the pot, just bought it from someone. I might be able to limit the charge to misdemeanor receiving stolen property. Since you have no formal record, it might be possible to get you out of this with no jail time."

I shook my head. "This is not Monopoly where you can land in jail by the roll of the dice. I don't need a 'get out of jail free' card."

"You might change your mind once we arrest you."

"That's a bluff and not a good one. You can't arrest me without evidence, and you don't have any because I didn't steal the pot."

He took half a step forward and stared at me. I tried to hold his gaze without looking defiant. He was six inches taller than me. His head was huge, his face flat. His round eyes protruded so far from their sockets that I thought a hearty slap on his back might pop them out.

With no change in expression, he added, "There could be a finder's fee."

"If I find the pot, you'll be the first person I call."

He left without saying goodbye. I noticed his hair was perfectly still as he stepped into the wind.

8

Miss Gladys Claiborne brought me lunch late that afternoon.

I told her I'd eaten an entire sack of breakfast burritos, but she was undeterred. "It's just a little ol' leftover casserole," she said as she smoothed an embroidered placemat onto my counter and fussily arranged a matching napkin on top of it. As she lowered the plate, I peered down at the concoction.

"What might this be called?"

"Back home we always called it Emma's Tuna because everybody learned the recipe from Emma Higginbotham. It was one of Mr. Claiborne's favorites."

Mr. Claiborne was her tubercular husband who died twenty years ago leaving her with a fortune made in the cotton futures business. She was called Miss Gladys even when she was married to him. The gift shop that bears her name is two doors to the west of me. She sells tea cozies, antimacassars and those horrid naked Indian girl statues made by the Frankoma Company near Tulsa.

"I can't remember a time when we sat down to Sunday dinner that my four-quart silver chafing dish wasn't full of Emma's Tuna. Except of course when Father Rice came for dinner, and then Mr. Claiborne always insisted on a standing rib roast."

"*Father* Rice? Are you Catholic, Miss Gladys?"

There was a quick intake of breath. "Why, heavens no. My people have been Episcopalians ever since Henry divorced Catherine."

I didn't tumble to who she was talking about. "Was Henry one of your ancestors?"

She giggled. "I do love your sense of humor. I'm speaking of Henry VIII, and I'm afraid we don't have a drop of royal blood. But if it hadn't been for King Henry, there wouldn't be any Episcopalians. Or Whiskeypalians as they called them in East Texas. The Baptists and the Methodists thought we were terrible sinners. Why, even some of the Presbyterians were teetotalers. I know this isn't a ladylike thing to say, but when we moved out here among all these Catholics, it was the first time I had ever been able to set foot in a liquor store without feeling guilty."

I looked down at the casserole and told her she shouldn't have gone to all that trouble.

"It was no trouble at all. You start with canned tuna. I always use solid albacore. Then you combine it with noodles, chopped green onions, a can of cream of mushroom soup and a package of grated cheddar and bake it in the oven." Her pale blue eyes sparkled as she added, "Since we moved out here, I sometimes put a can of green chili in it."

I took a forkful of it. It wasn't bad. But with every bite I kept thinking of all that mercury lodging in my brain.

"You don't have to wait around here, Miss Gladys. I'll bring your stuff back to you just as soon as I finish."

"Oh, I wouldn't want you to eat all alone."

"But shouldn't you be in your shop?"

"I just put up that little sign with the clock face on it saying when I'll be back. But I swear business is so slow, I don't even know why I bother."

I nodded in agreement.

"It does my heart good to see you eat. I just hate cooking for nobody but myself. You know what you need? A wife."

"I'd be honored to marry you."

She pushed her hand through the air at me. "You are a handsome devil, but I'm old enough to be your mother. By the way, who was that attractive young lady who was in your shop earlier?"

"I think she's a runaway."

"Oh, dear."

"I could be wrong."

"There seem to be so many sad young people these days. When Sarah and Zachary were children, all their little friends seemed so happy. If there was a sad child in all of East Texas, I didn't know about it. Of course families were closer then . . ."

I finished the casserole and offered to wash the dishes and return them to her. She wouldn't hear of it, so I walked her back to her shop.

I felt bloated as I returned. I seldom eat lunch. I believe in starting the day with a hardy breakfast, meaning loaded with carbohydrates, animal fats and red or green chili. I may eat an avocado or a mango during the day, but I usually don't have another meal until after the cocktail hour and often have both in the same chair.

Susannah had a date with Mr. West Coast, but I walked over to Dos Hermanas Tortillería at five anyway. As the name implies, it started out as a tortilla factory. In New Mexico, that means they sell mainly *tamales* and *posole*. And you probably thought they sold tortillas. Well, they sell a few, but the ones in the grocery stores are cheap and good, so most people no longer buy tortillas at a factory.

Tamales, on the other hand, are a pain in *la cola* to cook, so people buy them at their local tortilla factory. The ones at Dos Hermanas are to die for, and considering how much lard goes into the *masa*, that may be literally true. The *masa* in a Dos Hermanas *tamale* is like a Mexican Rolaids—it will absorb up to forty-seven times its weight in stomach acid. Or Drano for that matter.

Posole is another matter. Even people in New Hampshire know what a *tamale* is. But *posole* has not caught on outside of New Mexico, perhaps for good cause. It's a stew made with hominy, chili, oregano and tripe. Now tripe, contrary to what the sound of the word conjures up in your mind, is almost fat free, so it's healthier than lard. But I usually chose the *tamales* anyway. Better to die happy than thin.

9

Kids always think their mothers are beautiful. When maturity and experience disabuse us of that notion, we still think they look terrific. Maybe not like the movie stars we saw at age five, but with a character of face just as intriguing.

It's the same with hometowns. I thought Albuquerque was the most beautiful city in the world. Then I saw pictures of Venice and Kyoto and realized that my hometown was not a classic beauty. But I love its character and wouldn't trade its high desert and mountains for canals or cherry blossoms.

I love the thin dry air at a mile above sea level. I can stand on the banks of the Rio Grande and look up at the Sandias, rising another mile above the city, reaching over ten thousand feet into space. White capped in the winter, verdant in the spring with dark pines and light aspens, yellow and gold in the crisp autumn, the mountains shelter Albuquerque from the east, from its geography and from its history.

Albuquerque is not about pilgrims and turkeys. It's about Spaniards and chilies.

I played as a child in the trackless expanse of the West Mesa across the Rio Grande, hunting imaginary bad guys through the sage, creosote, mesquite and chamisa around the dunes and the cottonwoods and willows along the arroyos.

Then Intel built a chip factory across the river and my wilderness playground became a synthetic quilt of faux adobe suburbs. The Chamber of Commerce says it provides jobs, but most of them were filled by people who transferred here. So we got more people, more traffic, more bad architecture and more chips. Nothing against Intel, but I liked the West Mesa better when the chips out there were produced by cows.

Albuquerque owes its existence to geography. Tijeras Canyon is the northernmost snow-free pass through the Rockies and the road that snaked through it for centuries eventually became Route 66 and then Interstate 40. The old road is now the main east/west thoroughfare and is called Central Avenue, a name that makes up in accuracy what it lacks in imagination. Central runs from the mouth of the canyon west past the University, through downtown, past the south edge of Old Town, across the Rio Grande and onto the West Mesa.

I left Dos Hermanas, turned east on Central and headed to the Hyatt.

Downtown has been reinvented again, but they still don't have it quite right. It was Friday night and the action was heating up, teenagers and college students strolling the street and packing the bars and cafés. Albuquerque's latest campaign to revitalize downtown has focused on the Route 66 theme. No one downtown looked old enough to remember the highway or the show, but they were hell-bent, as the theme song said, "to get your kicks on route sixty-six."

As in every other American city, suburbs and shopping centers put an end to downtown as a place to shop. Our city fathers decided downtown could be revitalized with an arts focus. There are sculpture pieces on the sidewalks and markers explaining the original architecture of buildings, many of which no longer exist or have been irretrievably altered for the worst. Thankfully, the KiMo Theater was saved, and the ornate façade with its weird Egyptian/ Southwestern motif still causes students of architecture to pause and scratch their heads. It is now a center for performing arts.

The revitalization plan seems to be working to some extent. Downtown used to be deserted after five. Now it can be quite lively. But most of the evening denizens were not there for the art unless bars and discos are considered art venues.

I thought about Guvelly and Wilkes being in the same hotel and the possibility that Wilkes was an undercover federal agent. Maybe his attempt to lure me into stealing the pot from the Valle del Rio Museum was a ploy. My attorney with the lawyerly name of Layton Kent would no doubt counsel me that an unsolicited invitation to commit a crime would be entrapment, and the evidence would not be admissible in court. Then again, I would be the one incarcerated until Layton got around to coming to the jail to *habeas* my *corpus*.

On the surface, Guvelly seemed menacing, but a lot of that might be his appearance. I couldn't decide whether his gruffness stemmed from being a cop or simply from a lack of social skills. If he was smart enough to pass the civil service exam, he must have known I didn't steal the pot. I've heard that cops sometimes put the word on the street by rousting known criminals and letting the grapevine do its work. But so far as I was aware, there was no network of pot thieves. I was also curious about his second visit and his apparent desire to negotiate. Since I was going to the Hyatt anyway, I decided to pay him a surprise visit.

I veered off Central onto Tijeras, which runs at a slight angle to the otherwise orderly grid of downtown and leads directly to the Hyatt, the tallest hotel in New Mexico. Which is akin to being the world's tallest midget. The lobby resembled the modern version of a Middle Eastern bazaar, a jumble of scents, colors, noises and bedlam. The scent of coffee from Starbucks mixed with the popcorn smell from the bar. Music from a pianist in the lobby added melody to a percussion trio entertaining a group on the mezzanine. Light glinted off the brass and marble, not to mention the sequins in the gowns of heavyset ladies attending some sort of gala.

I felt vaguely safe in the anonymity of the crowd as I crossed through a lobby full of people with nametags on their lapels, entered one of the four elevators and punched 11. No one on floors two through ten wanted to go up, so I enjoyed a nonstop ride. I stepped out of the elevator into silence.

I don't know why, but I felt as though I were trespassing. Maybe it was the camera above the bank of elevators. The security I had felt in the crowded lobby evaporated as I stood unprotected and alone in an empty vestibule.

I studied the sign explaining the numbering system, turned right then left and soon arrived at 1118. I looked for more cameras, even while thinking *too late now*, but I didn't see any along the corridor.

I stood in front of the door for several minutes thinking. I could forget the whole thing and just walk away. Forget Wilkes, too. Play it safe. Go home without knocking on either door. Forget about the Museum. Forget about the Mogollon pot. Forget about the $25,000.

Hmm.

I knocked on the door. No response. I knocked again, this time loudly. Same result. I put my ear to the door and heard only the low hum one hears in large buildings. I returned to the elevators and punched the Down button.

A bank of phones hung on the wall in the lobby around the corner from the elevators. I lifted the receiver of the first one and dialed the three digits of Wilkes' room number. As I pressed the third button, I noticed a slot for depositing coins. It wasn't a house phone. It was a pay phone. I pressed the lever to break the connection and stood with the phone to my ear while I thought.

Did I want the front desk to buzz Wilkes? No. Better not to have anyone know I did any kind of business with Wilkes.

I returned to the elevators and ascended to the ninth floor.

10

I stood at Wilkes' door as I had stood at Guvelly's, indecisive like the character in *The Lady or the Tiger*. Which would Wilkes turn out to be?

A little voice advised me to go home. I didn't belong here. I told the little voice I needed the money. He replied that I didn't need it enough to go for jail for it.

I turned to leave.

Then I remembered what I think about money-grubbing museums and soulless professional anthropologists. I remembered my spiritual bond with ancient potters. Would they want their work in a glass cage? In a building that may as well be a crypt for the traffic it hosts?

The rationalization worked. I knocked on the door. Wilkes must have been standing right behind it because it flew open as my fingers were still straightening out of the fist I knocked with.

I jumped and Wilkes laughed. I felt foolish for an instant and then reassured. There was something about his easy manner and sly smile that made him seem harmless.

Yet I knew his project was fraught with danger. I tried to remain guarded without revealing it.

Except for the fact that he was in it, Wilkes' room appeared vacant. The door opened to a vestibule from which I glanced into the bathroom. It revealed no toothbrush, no towel on the floor, no sign that anyone had used the room since the last visit of the chambermaid. There was no sign of luggage. The bed was perfectly made. There was no glass of water on the nightstand, no book on the table between the two chairs. Maybe he was obsessively neat. Or maybe he was in a hotel room to trick me into thinking he was from out of town.

I broke the ice by asking, "Do you want to check to see if I'm wearing a wire?"

He was in twill pants with a sharp crease, a grey flannel shirt, and squarish work shoes. His beard looked freshly trimmed. The deep lines at the corners of his eyes eased gently upward as he answered my question. "Why would you be?"

I returned his half smile. "If you ask a law-abiding citizen to steal something, he might report it to the police who then might enlist that citizen to meet with you and get the offer on tape."

"Could happen," he admitted, "but I don't think so in this case."

"Why not?"

He pointed me to one of the winged chairs and I sat. He took the other one. "First, you're not a law-abiding citizen. No offense intended."

"None taken. But I'm generally law-abiding."

"I don't doubt that you are—generally. But I'm fairly certain your respect for the law doesn't extend to federal regulations regarding archaeological resources."

The chair was comfortable and the room pleasantly warm. "I like to think of it as civil disobedience," I told him, only half tongue-in-cheek.

"Civil disobedience?"

I shrugged. "Okay, I know it sounds self-serving, but I think breaking laws that are absurd is healthy."

"I agree. It's just that I associate civil disobedience with Gandhi or Martin Luther King, not with grave robbing."

I assumed a hurt look. "Grave robbing is a harsh term." I was tempted to tell him I'm too squeamish to even consider it. But I didn't because he was trying to hire me to steal a pot, and who wants a squeamish thief?

"But it's what you do," he asserted.

"It's what Howard Carter did. I collect pots, not mummies."

"There must be some pristine pots in Indian graves. They buried pots full of food with their dead so they'd have food on their journey to the other world."

"Some did. Some didn't. But it doesn't matter. I buy most of my stock from Indian potters. I can't afford to offend my suppliers."

"And let me guess—some of them are your best friends."

I didn't know whether to be offended. I couldn't tell whether he disliked Indians and was insulting me by assuming I felt the same way or whether he was making a joke at the expense of fools who say things like that.

Evidently he sensed I was wondering about the remark, so he said, "I know Martin Seepu."

Martin is a close friend. "How do you happen to know Martin?"

"I've tried a couple of times to get him to sell me one of his uncle's pots, but he won't do it. He says he only deals with you."

"He tell you I was a pot digger?"

"No, someone else told me that. What Martin told me was that you're a genius when it comes to Pueblo pottery. You can name the pueblo and the potter at a glance and copy their work to perfection."

"I never copy their work. I just copy ancient pots."

"Another case of not wanting to offend your suppliers?"

"Yeah, and the old stuff is more valuable anyway."

He laughed. "I used to turn up bones and pots by the ton. It's nice to say you don't dig in graves, but the whole planet is one big graveyard, Schuze."

He told me he had served in the Corps of Engineers. He was forced into early retirement, but he didn't say why. I ventured the opinion that involuntary retirement is better than being kicked out of school, but he didn't think so. Under his quiet and unassuming manner, there bubbled some anger.

"I oversaw drag line and bucket operations on projects all over the West," he said. "Every third scoop had an artifact in it. No one else cared, so why should I?"

His tone was not quite bitter—more resigned. After he was forced out, he began a second career in antiquities. I got the sense that he was like me, cashing in on the riches of the earth. The main difference was that I did my own digging whereas he benefited from Uncle Sam's heavy equipment.

I assumed his remark about the entire planet being a graveyard was hyperbole, but I told him that we were headed in that direction. Wasting space on graves is one of my pet peeves, like storing artifacts in museum basements. He asked why I was against graveyards, and I pointed out the practical issue that no one other than me seems to worry about; namely, that the number of people needing burial grows exponentially while the amount of land remains constant, so we're going to run out of space.

He cocked his head. "Cemeteries don't take that much space, do they?"

"Think about it. There are over six billion people alive today. Say a burial plot is ten feet by five. That's fifty square feet. Multiply that by six billion and you get three hundred billion square feet." I did a quick mental calculation. "That's over twelve thousand square miles. So to bury the current population will require more room than the entire of state New Jersey."

"And good riddance," he laughed. "But I see your point. Still, there are a lot of New Jersey–sized places around the world."

"Not so many as you might think. The earth is mostly water. Then you have to discount steep terrain, swamps and the frozen areas to the north and south. You also have to subtract areas already under some other use, land we grow food on, live on, build factories on, etc. If the current population growth trend continues, it will be a close call to see which we run out of first, food to feed the masses or burial space for them when they starve."

"You have a weird mind."

I shrugged in admission. "Things make more sense to me when I put numbers on them. I used to be an accountant." I finally got around to the concern I was harboring. "A federal agent came to my shop yesterday."

"Was his name Guvelly?"

I was surprised and relieved at how easily he asked the question. "How did you know?"

"I saw him in the lobby today. Our paths have crossed before."

"The card Guvelly gave me said he worked in the Santa Fe office. Why would someone whose office is just an hour away stay at a hotel here?"

Wilkes shrugged. "Just another example of the Federal Government's fraud, waste and abuse program?"

I laughed. Wilkes asked if I wanted a drink. I said I did and he called room service for a couple of beers. The two chairs were next to a large window on a south-facing wall. It had started to drizzle and the streetlights nine stories below had coronas.

While we were waiting, Wilkes returned to the topic of Guvelly. "I think he's investigating a theft from Bandelier. Someone stole a pot like the one we talked about."

"He thinks I stole it," I said.

"Did you?"

"No," I replied quickly. "Did you?"

He laughed. "No, but I understand why you might think so. It would be quite a coincidence if my asking you to get the pot from the Valle del Rio Museum and the disappearance of the one at Bandelier just happened to occur in the same time frame."

I nodded. The beers came. After Wilkes signed the tab, the room service guy left and Wilkes said, "As you probably guessed, I want the UNM pot for a client. When I heard about the theft at Bandelier, my first thought was my client had enlisted someone else to get that pot for him. I asked him about it, and he denied any involvement."

I said nothing. My first impulse was to believe him. But the coincidence was worrying.

After a brief silence, Wilkes asked, "Do you think you might come into possession of the pot we talked about?"

I didn't answer his question directly. Instead, I told him I visited the Museum.

"And?" he asked.

"It won't be easy."

"You have a plan?"

"I'm working on it," I said.

Sort of, I thought to myself.

11

It was late when I left the Hyatt. The rain had stopped, and the evening air was brisk. As I approached my shop, I saw something or someone wedged against the bottom of the door.

I stayed across the street in case it was a rabid dog or a mugger lying in wait. It was late, dark, cold and wet, and I guess my imagination got the best of me. As I drew near, I saw it was a person curled up asleep.

Except she wasn't asleep. She stood up and said, "Hi, Hubert."

"Kaylee, what are you doing here?"

"Can we go inside? It's freezing out here."

I unlocked the door and led her back to the kitchen where I started a pot of coffee. I sat her down in a chair and stood next to the kitchen counter.

"What's going on?"

"I don't have anywhere to go."

"Where do you live?"

"Nowhere."

"Where did you used to live?"

"What difference does that make?"

I pulled out a chair and sat in it facing her. "You must have waited for me because you wanted me to help you. And since you stayed out in the rain and cold by my door for hours, you must think you don't have any other options. Okay, I'm willing to help. But you have to cooperate."

A lot of dirt or grime had stuck to her thick makeup. When she wiped her sleeve across her face, it left a smear. Under the smear was a welt. She didn't say anything.

"Where did you used to live?"

"I didn't know you lived here," she said, ignoring my question and looking around my living quarters. "I was waiting for you to come in the morning and open your store."

"Kaylee, if you don't answer my questions, I can't help you."

"I'm not going to tell you where I lived."

"Then you'll have to leave," I said and stood up.

"Are you going to throw me out?"

"If I have to."

She gave my five six height and hundred forty weight a derisive look. "You're not very big."

"I'll call the police."

"I'm not going back there. You can't make me go back."

"I'm not trying to make you go anywhere. I just need to find out what your situation is."

She pouted for a moment and then put her head down. When she looked up again, she had a forced leering smile. "My situation is that I'm a woman. And you're a man. And we're all alone late at night in your house. Does that give you any ideas, Hubert?"

"Yes, it gives me the idea to call the police." I picked up the phone.

She started crying. "Please don't call them."

I kept dialing, but slowly.

"I'm from Texas," she said.

"Where in Texas?"

"Wildorado."

I put down the phone. "Where is that?"

"This side of Amarillo. It's famous for the feedlot smells."

"You left to get away from the smell?"

"Sure," she said unconvincingly.

"How long have you been in Albuquerque?"

"Three days."

"You ran away from home?"

"I'm not a teenager. I just decided to move to Albuquerque."

I sighed. "When people move, Kaylee, they usually have furniture or at least suitcases."

She looked at me hopefully. "I can get that stuff. If you hire me as a salesgirl, I could buy furniture and stuff."

"I don't need a salesgirl."

"Do you need a girlfriend?"

"No, I don't need a girlfriend either."

"You already have one? I don't care. I wouldn't say anything to her."

"We're not talking about me. We're talking about you. You're the one who needs help. Right now you need a place to stay, so you can sleep here tonight. In the morning, we'll figure out what to do next." I thought about my five-hundred-thread-count Egyptian long-staple cotton sheets. I have to admit I'm a bit fastidious. "You also need a shower."

"I don't have any clean clothes to put on."

"You didn't even bring . . . Never mind." I went to my chifferobe and took out a shirt and a pair of sweat pants. "Take these into the bathroom. Take off your clothes and throw them out here on the floor and then take a shower and put these on." I handed her the shirt and pants.

She followed my instructions. I guess I should have added that when she threw her dirty clothes out, she should stand behind the door while doing so.

"Jesus," I said, and looked away.

"Thanks, Hubie."

"Close the door and take a shower."

I put her clothes in the washer after I removed a worn billfold, some change and a half-eaten Snickers. I looked through her wallet. She was right about not being a teenager. Her driver's license showed her to be twenty-one. There was a picture of a young guy about her age, a ten, two ones and a horoscope card for Leos.

I put her wallet, belt, shoes and other meager belongings on the counter and started making *huevos rancheros*. I normally drink champagne with late night breakfasts, but the coffee was brewed, and I didn't think popping a cork was a good idea.

At least she knew how to shower. She looked clean and refreshed when she emerged, and she lit into the food like a dog. Without the heavy makeup and lipstick, the puffy lip and welt on her cheek were more noticeable. I decided not to ask.

I showed her to my bed and told her to get some sleep. She looked around the place. "Where are you going to sleep?"

"I have a hammock in the patio."

She giggled. "It's freezing out there. You could sleep with me." Started to unbutton the shirt I had given her.

"Keep the shirt on. If you try any more monkey business, I'm calling the cops."

I got my thermal underwear and knit hat from my chest of drawers and went to the bathroom where I put them on under my clothes. Then I got my sleeping bag and went out to the patio.

I'm an amateur astronomer, and I often sleep outside because I enjoy gazing up at the stars, although I normally choose warmer nights. Tonight I wasn't thinking about the heavens. I was wondering whether allowing Kaylee to stay was a good idea. The doors from my living quarters to the workshop and from there into the shop were deadbolted as they always are at night, so there was no danger she would break a pot. And what damage could she do in my living quarters? Rip my sheets? Steal my forks?

I decided not to worry about it. I looked up in the sky and remembered that Pythagoras was the first person to discover that the morning star and the evening star are one and the same, the planet Venus. I looked for Venus, but of course it had already passed the meridian at that late hour. The next thing I knew, so had I.

12

Kaylee slept late. When she awoke, I started fixing her another plate of *huevos rancheros*.

Someone knocked at the door just as I finished cooking, and I went forward to discover Whit Fletcher, Detective First Grade, Albuquerque Police Department. Fletcher is about six feet tall with silver hair always in need of a trim and blue-grey eyes that slant down and make him look tired. We've had a few dealings over the years, usually ending with me getting out of a jam and Whit getting money. I've never actually bribed him, but I have made it possible for him to supplement his income. He's not a bad cop. He goes after the drug dealers, wife-beaters, rapists and murderers with zeal. The American Civil Liberties Union would probably see it as a little too much zeal, but then Whit probably doesn't belong to the ACLU.

He doesn't have any interest in arresting pot thieves or people who forgot to get a license for a cat, and he's not above making a buck on the sly.

"Well, if it ain't Hubert Shoots, my favorite grave robber. I'm surprised to find you here, Hubert. I thought you would be on the lam by now."

"It's 'Schuze.' Sounds like what you wear on your feet."

"Which is exactly what you should be putting to work walking yourself away. But here you are in your little fencing operation as usual."

"Where else should I be?"

"As far away as possible. That's where I'd be if I'd murdered someone."

"Well, you didn't murder anyone and neither did I."

"That's what I told 'em downtown. I said to 'em, 'He steals pots. He don't murder people.' But unfortunately, they got witnesses that put you at the scene."

The trembling came on unexpectedly, as if my autonomous nervous system got the message before it reached my conscious mind. I put my hands on the counter so he wouldn't see them shaking. I asked what scene he was referring to, and of course he said it was the Hyatt.

"You were there weren't you?"

"I was. But I didn't murder anyone."

"Well, what were you doin' there? You weren't attending that convention, where you?" He flipped open a small notebook and consulted his notes. "It's called the Philadelphia Society."

"Philadelphia Society?"

"Yeah, they collect stamps. Funny name for a bunch of stamp collectors. Maybe they only collect stamps from Pennsylvania. You weren't there as a stamp collector, were you?"

"No, I wasn't. I just went to have a drink with a friend."

"Your friend a man or a woman?"

"A man."

"Meet him at the bar, did you?"

"No, I went to his room. He's a guest there." My mind was racing. Had someone killed Carl Wilkes?

"Your friend got a name?"

"I don't think I should give you his name."

"Why not? He won't be needing it if he's dead."

"I don't know if he's dead. I don't want to violate his privacy by giving his name to the police when he hasn't done anything wrong to the best of my knowledge."

"Okay, don't give me his name. He'll just have to stay John Doe until we find out who he is. And I'll tell you what I'm gonna do because you and me are friends, Hubert. I'm going to tell you his room number. It's 1118. Was that your friend's room?"

So it was Guvelly. He was a jackass, but that didn't mean he deserved to be murdered.

"No. I'm happy to say that my friend was not in room 1118."

"Maybe in an adjoining room?"

"No," I said, "he was on an entirely different floor."

He leaned against my counter and smiled. "So maybe you can explain what you was doing on the eleventh floor?"

I started to deny it then remembered the security camera near the elevator.

"I guess I pushed the wrong button."

Fletcher stared at me while he used one of his big meaty hands to push his hair out of his eyes. "I guess that could happen. There's lots of buttons in those elevators in big buildings. Who woulda thought we'd ever have skyscrapers in Albuquerque?" He shook his head in apparent wonderment and his hair fell back over the eye. Then he stared at me.

"Well," I said, "even if I was unlucky enough to accidentally be on the floor where someone was murdered, at least I wasn't there when the murder took place."

He shook his head. "That's exactly when you were there. We got a little piece of evidence that times you and ties you in real tight, but I can't tell you about it even though you and me are friends."

I stood there with my mind racing, wondering what the other piece of evidence might be, trying to remember if I had done anything that seemed perfectly innocuous at the time but might now look suspicious to police investigators.

And that's when Kaylee walked in flashing cleavage in my loose-fitting shirt and holding a bottle of Gruet *Blanc de Noir* in her right hand.

"Can we open this?"

Whit's eyebrows arched up. "Who's the young lady, Hubert?"

"Whit, this is Kaylee. Kaylee, meet Whit Fletcher," I said, and added without thinking, "from the Albuquerque Police Department."

Whereupon she gave me a look of betrayal, threw the champagne bottle at me and ran back to my living quarters. She tried to lock the door, but I got there in time to force it open, and Whit was right behind me.

She slumped down in a chair and started crying.

Fletcher gave me his stern cop look. "What the hell's going on here?" He turned to Kaylee. "How old are you, Miss?"

"She's twenty one," I said.

"You better hope so."

"Oh, come on, Whit. Give me a little credit, huh. She showed up her last night with nowhere to go, so I told her she could stay and then we'd figure out what to do this morning."

"With her shirt half off and a bottle of booze in her hand, it looks like she figured out exactly what to do. You sure she's over eighteen?"

She was continuing to sob and didn't say anything.

"I'm sure," I said.

"Well, I've got some more questions for you," he said.

"I've already told you everything I know about her."

"I'm not talking about her. I'm talking about what happened at the Hyatt."

Funny how the mind works. I found myself entertaining the irrational hope that this was a dream and I would wake up. Then I found myself wondering if we could start over. I almost asked Fletcher if he would step outside, come in again and let me have another shot at our conversation.

But of course I didn't. Instead I said, "Maybe I should talk to my lawyer before I say anything else."

"We got a telephone downtown. You can call him when we get there."

13

Fletcher let me call Susannah before we left, and she promised to pick up Kaylee.

On the way downtown, I decided the smart thing was to say nothing until my lawyer arrived. And just as a change from my recent string of decisions, I decided to do the smart thing.

I spent an eternity in a windowless room with a metal table and four chairs. I asked for something to read, but that request was denied. I asked for a glass of water and was given one. I thought about asking for bread to go with the water, but decided against it.

I hadn't killed Guvelly. I hadn't entered his room. Perhaps my fingerprints were on the outside of his door. Surely fingerprints on the *outside* of a door are not enough evidence to convict someone of committing a murder *inside* the room. I would let Layton handle everything. There was nothing to worry about.

Except paying his bill. He is the most expensive attorney in town. Of course if I stole the pot at UNM and Wilkes paid me twenty-five thousand . . . What was I thinking? Here I was at the police station being questioned for murder, and I was considering committing a burglary to pay for my defense. And I'm not even a burglar. Unless I had beginners' luck, I'd probably be caught in the act.

Layton Kent, Esquire, finally showed up and carted me away in his Rolls. He has an office downtown but conducts most of his business from his table overlooking the 18th green at his club.

Layton and his wife, Mariella, are one of the most prominent couples in town. Many of his clients are fellow lawyers who use him to set up corporations, trusts and other scams for their ill-gotten but perfectly legal gains.

Despite the nature of his practice, Layton condescended to spring me from jail because Mariella, said to be a descendent of Don Francisco Fernández de la Cueva y Enríquez, *Duque de Albuquerque*, is an avid collector of traditional Native American pots, and I am her personal dealer. Whether she is in fact descended from *El Duque* is subject to debate. However, Ms. Kent is a nice lady, and it would be ungallant to question her lineage. Not to mention bad for business.

My trim behind and Layton's ample one had just hit the leather seats of his table when we were surrounded by other diners wanting to make sure they were seen with and by Layton. Solicitous staff placed chilled flutes in front of us and cloth napkins on our laps.

The cadaverous-looking captain appeared with a bottle of Dom Pérignon and said, "Shall I pour, Mr. Kent?"

"Yes, Phillip, please."

Layton sipped the champagne and indicated his satisfaction with a long sigh. I was hoping to be included in this largess and was not disappointed. Dom Pérignon may be a notch or two above New Mexico's own Gruet, but it costs a hundred dollars a bottle. I stick to the Gruet, which is available for thirteen bucks at the discount store and tastes almost as good.

Although Layton weighs three hundred pounds, he is light on his feet and has only one chin, albeit a very large one that extends from his jaw to the bottom of his neck without any sign of an Adam's apple. He was wearing a taupe wool suit with a gold silk tie and matching handkerchief. The collar of his hand-tailored shirt rolled in such a way that it seemed to embrace his neck, creating a snug fit without allowing any of Layton's skin to hang over the collar.

"Chef Marcel has sage hens today, Mr. Kent," said Phillip.

"Excellent. We'll both have that."

I was never offered a menu.

"We're having chicken with sage?" I asked in surprise. Sage is an excellent herb for fowl, but the menu at Layton's club runs more to *haute cuisine.*

"They are not chickens, Hubert. They are sage hens. They are relatives of the grouse and live in and feed off the sage in Wyoming so that they have a natural sage flavor unlike anything that can be imparted by applying herbs externally to a domestically raised bird."

"Oh."

"Marcel usually stuffs them with morels, but it may be too early in the year for morels. In that case, he may have some porcini. Also excellent, though I prefer the morels."

I would prefer Consuela's chicken enchiladas, I thought to myself.

"Now," he continued, "tell me who you are thought to have murdered and why they think it."

I told him almost the whole story—Wilkes coming to my store and tempting me to steal the Mogollon water jug from the Valle del Rio Museum, Guvelly coming to my store and accusing me of stealing the other Mogollon water jug from Bandelier and my visit to the Hyatt, both the eleventh and the ninth floors. I know you're supposed to tell your lawyer everything, but I didn't tell him about my visit to the Museum.

Our sage hens arrived, stuffed with morels, and I admit they were delicious. Layton doesn't discuss business while he eats, so we were both able to enjoy the meal. He ordered mango-scented flan for desert. I declined. We got back to business over coffee.

"I don't understand why the police don't know the name of the victim. The innkeepers statute in this state is quite clear. Every guest must be registered under his or her true and legal name. You say this Guvelly showed you his badge?"

"Yes, but I didn't get a good look at it."

"You should have insisted. There might be a problem with his identity, which would explain why the authorities haven't formally charged you."

"How so?"

"They may have discovered he is not who he represented himself to be. They can charge you with murder without knowing the name of the victim, but it makes getting a true bill from the grand jury more difficult. So they could be trying to identify him before formally charging you."

"They might arrest me again?"

"You were not arrested. You were merely detained. And if they do arrest you or make any contact with you, you must notify me immediately. And for God's sake, say absolutely nothing."

14

Miss Gladys Claiborne must have been watching for me because just moments after I got home, she showed up with a dish she called Chicken Delight. Odds are it was dreamed up by an elegant Texas woman named Delight.

The dish centers on chicken tenders, a piece of the chicken I am not familiar with. The tenders are combined with canned French-cut green beans, cream of chicken soup and a crust made of crumbled shoestring potatoes from a can. Yum.

I begged off on the grounds of my large lunch with Layton. But I made the mistake of telling the truth when she asked if I had eaten dessert, so I had to agree to eat the rectangle of lime Jell-O with crushed pineapple and miniature marshmallows.

I remembered Susannah telling me that Jell-O has something in it that's good for you, so with that in mind I took a few forkfuls.

"A very rude man came to my shop the other day, Mr. Schuze. He works for the government, and I'm certain he must be a Yankee because he had no manners to speak of."

"Was his name Guvelly?"

"I believe it was. I could scarcely understand him when he spoke."

"Did he say he was investigating me?"

"I'm not supposed to tell you that," she said and winked.

"Well, he accused me of stealing a pot from Bandelier, but I didn't."

"Of course you didn't. And it was rude of him to talk to your neighbors behind your back. I told him so. I also told him there's not a reason in the world why you would steal a pot. You can make any pot you want. You are so talented."

"Thank you. And thanks for telling me about Guvelly coming to see you."

"I just hope he doesn't return," she said.

I told her that was unlikely. I didn't tell her the reason was that he was dead.

15

A brief shower dampened my Windbreaker as I crossed the plaza, but it disappeared as I reached Dos Hermanas as if to remind me of our capricious spring weather.

The freshet dropped the temperature into the fifties, so I kept my jacket zipped up to my neck. The Dom Pérignon hadn't completely worn off, and poor Margarita was languishing on the table unsipped.

Susannah was wearing jeans, a Western shirt and a quilted vest. "You want to tell me about your new girlfriend?"

I was still thinking about the pending murder charge. I looked at her blankly. Then it came to me. "Kaylee?"

"She's attractive in an earthy sort of way. I imagine you two had quite a time last night."

I shook my head. "It was quite a time alright. I had to threaten her with the police, wash her clothes and feed her. Then this morning she threw a champagne bottle at me."

"A lovers' spat so early in the relationship?"

"Lovers' spat? Don't even kid about it. Whit Fletcher was there when she threw the champagne, and he started asking me about her age because he thought . . . well . . ."

She leaned back in her chair and smiled. "I know what he thought. And according to Kaylee, he was right."

"What do you mean?"

"She said she slept with you."

"What! That's completely—"

"Calm down. I know you didn't."

Forget the lingering Dom Pérignon. I took a large sip of my margarita. "She actually said that?"

"Actually, she said she slept in your bed. But it was obvious she wanted me to think you were in it with her."

"Why would she say that?"

"Judging from the marks on her face, she's had an unfortunate relationship with a man. She's alone and broke with nowhere to go. You take her in, feed her, let her get cleaned up and give her a warm place to sleep. She doesn't know how to relate to men except through sex and violence. You're not violent, so that leaves sex."

"I thought you stopped majoring in psychology."

"You don't have to be a psychologist to realize she sees you as a safe haven. And in her world, the only way to make sure she can stay with you is to give you her body."

"Well, she can keep it. Where is she?"

"I turned her over to Father Groaz."

"Good move. He'll know what to do, and I won't have to deal with her."

"I wouldn't be so sure of that."

"Why do you say that?" I asked warily.

"Because any place he puts her, a shelter for example, won't be as appealing as you and your house. When she gets the chance, she'll come back to you. It's like feeding a stray cat. They always come back."

"Oh, great."

We ordered a second round. I didn't care if it tasted as good as the first one. I took a refreshing gulp.

I sat there staring into the fire and then realized after a moment that Susannah was talking.

". . . like a fairy tale. We gazed into each other's eyes over drinks, shared a romantic meal and danced until the band went home . . ."

Then I remembered that while I had been fending off Kaylee, she had been fending off the LA guy.

". . . and then went back to his hotel where he started a fire."

Maybe *fending off* was not the right phrase. I wondered what sort of fire she was referring to.

Luckily, she didn't attempt to tell me what happened next. Instead she said, "He may be the one."

"I hope so."

"Do I detect some doubt?"

"I just don't want you to get hurt. I'm glad the two of you are off to a great start. But he's in Los Angeles and you're in Albuquerque. Long distance romances can be tricky."

She laughed. "How would you know? You've never been out of New Mexico."

"I went to Mexico once."

"You went to Juarez, part of which borders on New Mexico."

"But I went through El Paso, and that's in Texas."

She sighed. "Hubie, this is not a discussion about your travels or lack thereof. But you're right about long distance romances. And he understands that. He said we should start slow and see how things progress. He'll be stopping here every few weeks as his travel schedule allows, and we'll see how things develop."

"Sounds like a good idea."

I put my finger in my margarita and swirled the ice counterclockwise.

"Geez, you don't sound exactly thrilled about my new romance."

"Sorry. I'm a little preoccupied tonight."

"Still worried about Kaylee?"

"No," I said and told her everything that had happened that day.

"Wow. Gravelly is dead?"

"Guvelly," I corrected.

"Yeah, him. I've never known anyone who was murdered. Of course, I didn't actually know Gubelly. But I know you and you knew him, and I guess that's like what, two degrees of separation?"

"I don't understand that degrees of separation thing. But I know what you mean, and that's what bothers me. If someone you know is murdered, then the murderer might also be someone you know, like you've fallen into the wrong crowd."

"You didn't fall into Gubelly. He came to you."

"Guvelly. Here's what worries me. Obviously they know I was on the eleventh floor because of the camera by the elevator. And maybe they know I was at his door because I might have left fingerprints. That's just bad luck. But Fletcher said, 'We got a little piece of evidence that times you and ties you in real tight.' What do you think that might be?"

Susannah drained her glass and thought about it. I signaled to Angie for two more and held the chip bowl aloft to indicate we needed a refill on those as well.

After we were reprovisioned, Susannah said, "Maybe someone looked through the peephole when you knocked and saw you there."

I liked the initial sound of it and wondered why I hadn't thought of it. Then I saw the flaw in it.

"That would only implicate me if the person who saw me through the peephole did so at or near the time of the murder."

"Right."

"So who would be in the room at the time of the murder?"

"The murderer and the victim. Oh, I see what you mean. The victim can't report seeing you because he's dead. And the murderer can't report seeing you without implicating himself."

"But the peephole theory could still work."

"You mean if someone in another room looked out?"

"Exactly. I knocked twice and rather loudly the second time. So if someone across the hall heard the noise and looked out, they might have seen me."

"So what good does it do knowing that?"

Her question finally jostled my brain into gear, and I felt optimistic for the first time since Fletcher's visit to my shop. "If someone else saw me in the hall, then they might also have seen me walk away without going in."

"But how can you find out what room and who it was?"

"Maybe I can get Fletcher to tell me."

"He's a cop. Why would he help the suspect?"

"It's Whit Fletcher, Suze."

"Oh, of course—money."

"Exactly."

By that time, I had forgotten all about the Dom Pérignon I'd had at lunch. I drained my margarita.

16

I walked unsteadily back to my shop, let myself in the front door, heard the bong, made a silly joke to myself about a bong in a pot shop—well, I had been drinking—locked the front door behind me, used a different key to unlock the door to my workshop directly behind the store, relocked that, and then unlocked the next door in the series, the one into my living quarters.

At least that's what I thought I did.

My bed is a single, dressed, as you already know, with five-hundred-thread-count sheets of Egyptian long-staple cotton. After four margaritas, it was between those sheets that I longed to be. As tempting as it was simply to remove my shoes and crawl in, I forced myself to take a hot shower, two aspirins and a large glass of water. When finally my body slid between those millions of tiny threads, I was asleep in an instant.

I awoke many hours later refreshed and famished, thankful for the two benefactors of humankind who invented the margarita and the aspirin. I set the oven on warm and placed a plate inside with two corn tortillas. I broke two eggs into the frying pan and cooked them over-medium with a pinch of cumin. I placed the eggs over the tortillas, poured on green chili sauce, sprinkled *queso fresco* on top and returned the plate to the oven. While the cheese melted, I extracted a bottle of Gruet *Blanc de Noir* champagne from the fridge and filled a flute.

Why not? Hair of the dog. I then sat at my kitchen table and enjoyed my favorite breakfast—*huevos rancheros verde* and champagne.

While I ate, I read another article from the anthology about Pythagoras. I wondered what Pythagoras would make of my living space that has no right angles. Everything is slightly off, the walls akilter, the floors atilt. Pythagoras was evidently a man of precision. He and his cult worshipped numbers. The number one was God—perfect unity. Two was the duality of reality—man and woman, hot and cold, wet and dry, etc. He's even credited with discovering that harmony between plucked strings is a function of their length, so music is also a matter of numbers.

Despite all the precision of his famous theorem and his fixation with numbers, Pythagoras also had a mystical side. He taught that when you arise from sleep, you should smooth out the sheets lest someone use your imprint to harm you—sort of the early Greek root of the voodoo theory that you can injure someone by sticking a pin in their likeness. I glanced to my bed and saw my imprint. In a fanciful mood, I stepped over and smoothed it out. It was then that I heard someone moving about in my store. I looked at my watch and was surprised to see it was just past my normal opening time.

I opened the door into my workshop and heard someone calling my name from inside the shop. Reassured by the familiar voice, I unlocked the door from the workshop to the store and said good morning to Reggie West from next door. He sells gelato, which so far as I can tell is sherbet. It's even harder to sell during the off-season than pots because it faces the added challenge of being a summertime treat. Reggie has been trying to diversify into chocolates, piñon nut candies and jalapeño lollipops. They're better than they sound. Even with these exotic additions, I think he's struggling. Of course the alimony may also be a factor. Did I mention he pays it to two former wives? It's sad to see a former Marine laid low by family court.

"I noticed your lights were off even though it's past opening time, so I tried the door and it was unlocked. I thought you might be making pots, so I was just headed back to tell you to turn on the lights and put out the open sign."

"I thought I locked the door when I came in last night."

"Did you and Susannah close up Dos Hermanas again?"

"Yes, but I didn't think I was tipsy enough to leave the door unlocked."

"Well, I had my key to your shop in my hand, but the knob turned when I took hold of it, so I just walked in. Maybe it didn't quite catch when you turned the key last night."

I asked him to stay while I looked around to see if anything was missing. I have about a quarter of a million dollars of inventory, retail value, in my shop. Two thirds of it is in display cases or on shelves. None of that was missing. The rest of the merchandise is locked in cabinets behind my counter. I checked the cabinet doors, and they were all locked. However, a few of the hinges were slightly loose, and I was afraid someone had opened the cabinets by unscrewing the hinges. I unlocked each cabinet. Nothing was missing.

"Everything okay?" asked Reggie. He has a square face, a prominent chin and a smile that is so wide and bright it seems almost practiced.

"Seems to be. You mind keeping an eye out? In the unlikely case a customer comes along and wants to see something, just tell them I'll be back later."

After washing up the breakfast dishes and myself, I set off to Tristan's apartment. He's not actually my nephew. He's the grandson of my Aunt Beatrice, my mother's sister. I think that makes Tristan my second cousin once removed. Or maybe it's my first cousin twice removed. I've never been certain about the terminology. So I just call him my nephew, and he calls me his uncle.

He was asleep of course—it being prior to noon. I took along the only alarm clock that works, a steaming cup of aromatic coffee and a bag of pungent breakfast tacos from Duran Central Pharmacy.

During other hours of the day and most of the night, you can reach Tristan on an i-thingy. You can do almost anything on it—listen to music, play games, swamp the Internet and even have old-fashioned phone conversations. You can. Tristan can. I can't. I couldn't even figure out how to turn it on.

I let myself into his apartment with my key and held the coffee and tacos under his nose until he came to. He stared up at me. "Uncle Hubert?"

"Who were you expecting?" I stuck the food even closer to him.

"What time is it?" he asked groggily.

"It's time for breakfast."

He wrapped the blanket around himself like a cape, stood up and stretched. Then he flopped back into bed. At least he landed sitting up.

I handed him the coffee and he took a few tentative sips. Then he started in on the tacos. Once the chili and egg combo hit his taste buds, he was awake.

After he finished off the tacos, he wiped his mouth on the sheet and reached for what was left of the coffee.

"I could have gotten you a napkin," I said.

He shrugged. "I'm planning to wash the sheets today."

"I guess that means you have a date tonight."

"Yeah. I might even vacuum."

"You don't own a vacuum."

"I have a little hand-held one in the car."

"That one plugs into the cigarette lighter. Will the cord stretch all the way in here?"

"No, I rigged up a transformer. Then all I had to do was split the—"

"Tristan?"

"Oh, right. Not interested in technical things."

"Not usually, but I do have a technical question for you."

He smiled that big dopey smile the girls all love and said, "You didn't come over just to bring me breakfast?"

"Well, that too. And also just to visit." I really like the kid. He's sort of lost in space sometimes, but he's honest, smart, unassuming and really good with older people. And I don't mean me. I mean really old people. Of course the young girls also like him. With his vestigial layer of baby fat, smooth olive skin, black hair that hangs down in ringlets around his neck and those bedroom eyes, they find him irresistible.

"What's the question?"

"It's about the laser device on my shop door."

"It's basically harmless, but you shouldn't look directly into it. That's why it's mounted only three feet off the floor. If it were at shoulder height and you just happened to look to your right as you entered, it could contact your eyes and cause a problem. Also, it's not a good idea for it to pass real close to a pacemaker."

"I'll post a sign outside warning midgets with pacemakers to call ahead for special entry requirements. Why three feet high, by the way, instead of even lower?"

"It's hard for the average person to step over something three feet tall, so no one can enter undetected."

"Interesting, but not what I want to know. Can it keep a record of how many customers come in and when?"

"It not only can, it does. It's designed to hook into your business software so you can track exactly how many customers are in the store at different times of the day and make staffing decisions and things like that. Of course you don't have business software or even a computer, so the only feature you use is the sound that lets you know when someone enters or leaves."

"And the only staffing decisions I make are whether to open for business or not. So I couldn't find out how many people came in yesterday?"

"Sure you can. You don't use that function, but it's still in there. All you have to do is hook a computer to it and read the record off the memory chip."

"All I have to do? I can't understand what you said, much less do it."

He said he would take the reading for me. Before I left, I asked if he needed money. He said he was okay, so I gave him a fifty. When he says he's broke, I give him a hundred. When he says he's fine, I don't know what I give him because he's always either broke or just okay.

17

Susannah's idea about the peephole had me thinking I might work something out with Whit Fletcher. So when I got back from Tristan's, I called, and he came over.

"You decide to confess, Hubert?"

"Good afternoon, Detective. Nice to see you, too."

"Got any coffee?"

"It's just plain coffee," I told him. "If you want something fancy, there's a Flying Star over on Silver and a Starbucks in the Hyatt."

He took a sip. "You know what those places charge for a cup of coffee? Three dollars. You believe that? That can you got there probably didn't cost you three dollars."

He took another sip and sat the cup on the counter. "How come you don't keep no stools up here? Might be nice to take a load off."

Whit weights around two twenty, some of it in a paunch, but he seems in reasonable shape. His long face has a matching thin nose between those slant-down eyes.

"I don't want customers sitting at the counter drinking coffee. I want them browsing around the shop selecting purchases."

"What do you care? You don't make no money in here. This place is just a front for the illegal stuff you sell on the sly."

I didn't comment on that. Instead, I told him about the missing pot from Bandelier and about a federal agent making two visits to my shop.

"So why are you tellin' me? Bandelier ain't exactly in my jurisdiction."

I told him my theory. The federal agent didn't really think I stole the pot. I don't break into buildings. But the thief might bring it to me because of my reputation. The agent hoped to scare me enough that I would give him the pot to avoid trouble.

Whit drained the last of his coffee, wiped his mouth with the back of his hand and put his cup on the counter. "That's a nice fairy tale, but I don't understand why you're tellin' me about it?"

"The agent said there may be a finder's fee, but I can't collect it, can I?"

"Probably not. A thief don't usually get a finder's fee for returning what he stole."

"I didn't steal it. But they aren't going to believe that if I walk in with it under my arm."

He brushed his hair back and smiled. "And that's where I come in."

Whit's quick to pick up the scent of money.

"Exactly. If I can find the pot, I can pass it on to you to collect the fee."

"And we split it."

"Naturally, I would want something for my effort in recovering the thing."

"Naturally. But you're forgetting one thing. If your story is right, this federal agent might be after that fee, and he's not gonna take too kindly to you throwing it my way rather than his."

It was time for me to put my ace on the table. "I don't think we'll have a problem with the agent." I played a drum roll in my head and said, "His name is Guvelly, the guy in room 1118."

He picked up the cup to take another sip, saw that it was empty and put it back down. Then he just stood there thinking. Finally, he said, "If I remember right, Hubert, you told me you went up to room 1118 by mistake."

So much for my dramatic announcement.

"I lied. Guvelly told me he was in the Hyatt. He seemed to be trying to snare me. So I decided to drop in on him unannounced. I went up to the eleventh floor. No one answered my knock."

"You just stood outside the door."

"Right."

"Un huh. You hear a shot while you was standin' there?"

"I didn't hear anything."

Fletcher's eyes drooped further down than normal. "Maybe you oughta think about your story some more and then give me a call."

I'm usually happy to see Fletcher go, but this time I wished he had stayed for two reasons. First, I wanted to know why he didn't react to my knowledge that Guvelly was the murder victim. Second, I needed him to protect me from the two Indian thugs who walked into my shop after he left.

The first one looked like someone you'd encounter at the top of a beanstalk. He was a foot taller than me, and any one of his limbs outweighed me. His face was a random assortment of planes circling two small eyes. I thought he was alone until I heard someone behind him close the door and turn the latch.

I leaned over to see a bowling ball of a man so thick around the chest that his arms stuck out like a penguin's wings. He was short like me and looked as wide as he was tall. He stood fast against the door he had just locked.

The larger one reached the counter and, somewhat to my surprise, demonstrated the power of speech. "We want the pot back."

"Which one?" I croaked.

"The one from Bandelier. But we don't want it in the white man's museum."

I said nothing, partly because I didn't know what to say and partly because I had developed a sudden case of dry mouth.

I think he was looking at me, but I couldn't be sure because the slits that passed for eyes were almost closed. He looked like one of those heads from Easter Island, slightly smaller but with about as much animation.

"You understand?" he asked.

I nodded.

He reached over to the nearest shelf and picked up a small pot. It sat in his hand like a peanut in a catcher's mitt. Then he slammed it down on the counter.

The sound of the pot shattering was like the crack of a rifle shot, and I jumped like a deer in the crosshairs.

When I landed, the little black and white Acoma pot was a pile of shards.

I hated being threatened, but I hated what he did to the pot even more. It wasn't all that rare. You can buy a new one like it at Acoma for five hundred dollars on any day they allow tourists in. But seeing the pieces on my counter made me sad.

I recovered a bit of courage. "Why did you do that?"

He handed me a card and the two thugs left without comment left. The card had the likeness of Kokopelli on it and read *firstNAtions*.

18

I don't have nerves of steel. More like silver, a finer and more malleable metal.

So I was still jumpy after they left. It was only three, but I closed the shop anyway and went for a walk to settle down. As the rabbit said to Alice, "If you don't know where you're going, any path will take you there."

I turned east on Central because I didn't want to face the afternoon sun. I went through downtown, under Interstate 25 and stopped in front of Albuquerque High School.

Or what used to be Albuquerque High School. It was built in 1914 with red brick walls and granite lintels and pediments. Its classical style and proportions are reminiscent of a Greek temple, befitting the lofty purpose for which it was built. For sixty-five years it served that purpose well. Then I graduated and they abandoned it.

I don't think there was a causal connection.

The building was boarded up for years, but it's now been

chopped up into lofts. I stood on the sidewalk staring as nostalgia reached out from under the shallow facelift and tugged me back.

We were the "Mighty Bulldogs." I was one of those strange kids who spent more time in the library than at the games. When I did watch the football or basketball team, I couldn't see why everyone got so worked up. They're just games and strange ones at that. How serious can you be about ten guys running around in their undershirts tossing a ball at a basket? And to top it off, the drawing of our mascot in those days didn't look mighty. He looked like one of those dogs from the Coolidge paintings, playing poker with other breeds and smoking cigars.

But I was happy and the world benevolent. Life was simple back then. People didn't walk into shops and smash the merchandise.

The current Albuquerque High School on the extension of Indian School Road does a good job for all I know. But it looks like it a Walmart. They have a website, an attendance policy, a dress code and a mission statement. When I was in high school, everyone knew how to dress and the attendance policy was three words: go to school. The moment those words came to me, I could hear in my head my father's voice saying them.

God, I'm starting to sound just like him.

Nostalgia is like quicksand—if you wiggle around in it, it can pull you down. But it can also be calming. I realized I didn't have to put up with thugs. I didn't have to be in the business I was in. I didn't have to be in any business. With the way Old Town property has inflated, I could sell my place and live off the interest.

I looked at my watch and was pleased to note that if I walked back to Old Town at my normal pace, it would be happy hour when I got there.

19

"You can't be serious about closing."

"I am serious. First Carl Wilkes comes into my shop and asks me to steal a pot. Then Guvelly comes in and accuses me of stealing one. Then Fletcher comes in and accuses me of murder. And to top it all off, I'm visited by the Indian versions of Sacco and Vanzetti."

Susannah had told me about her day at La Placita. She'd had the usual mixture of locals and tourists, but no one had smashed anything. She waved toward Angie.

"You sure you want another one?"

"I don't have class tonight and Kauffmann is lecturing on the east coast."

"Kauffmann?"

"My LA hunk."

"What's his first name?"

"That is his first name."

"Oh."

"You don't like his name?"

"I didn't say that. It's just a bit unusual."

"Yeah? Well let me tell you, Hubert, I've dated a lot of guys named Sam or Charlie, and having a normal name doesn't mean you're a nice guy."

I sipped at my margarita.

"Sorry," she said, "I didn't mean to snap at you."

The warm wind from the south had sent us out to the veranda. The sand it carried sent us back in.

"What would you do if you closed the shop? Would you get an honest job?"

"I had an honest job once."

"Working as an accountant, right? That doesn't sound too honest these days. You didn't do any work for Enron did you?"

"It was a local firm. We didn't have any accounts big enough to cheat for."

"Why did you leave?"

"Two years of preparing financial statements under the watchful eye of one of the partners. Like a nine to five wake."

"What about the other young guys? Weren't any of them fun to work with?"

"Like arrows flying straight and true towards partnerships. I knew I wasn't going to make it. I knew deep inside I didn't want to."

"What about nights and weekends."

"We took work home most nights. On the weekends, I studied for the CPA exam, which I never took. Then I was at a strip mall one day and saw a shop called Feats of Clay."

"And you went in anyway?"

"Embarrassing to remember. I took a class along with eight blue-haired ladies. We painted and fired prefabricated bisque."

"So that's how you became a potter?"

"It was a start. It got me back in college. Driving by the campus one day, I realized I'd missed out on college. I attended, but I didn't really have the college experience."

"I've been having it for years, Hubie. It's not all that great."

"But that's my point. You're still trying different subjects. I started out in math and then everyone told me there was no future in that, so I switched to accounting. I did well enough, but I never felt any passion for it. So I went back and started over."

"At least you found your field right away. As a student, I've had more incarnations than Shirley MacLaine."

"Maybe art history is what you've been searching for."

"I'm not sure what I can do with it, but I enjoy the ideas. I bet you felt the same way about anthropology?"

"I started back in art because of the pots. But I soon realized that it was the designs that fascinated me. I took an anthropology course called something like 'Southwestern Pueblo Cultures' just to learn more about pots, and I was hooked on anthropology."

"But you don't just study pots—you make them."

I nodded. "There's power in throwing a pot, even a copy. The earth—okay, it's just a little clump of earth, but I always think of it as the earth—follows your fingers, its shape widening as you press outwards, its height extending as you urge it upwards. There's something almost sexual about the clay and how it changes shape under your touch."

She gave me a coy smile. "You need to start dating."

I laughed.

She changed the subject and asked me about my conversation with Whit Fletcher and whether he took the bait of the finder's fee.

"No, but he saw it coming fast enough."

"Does it bother you dealing with a crooked cop?"

"There's not much in life that's perfect. He doesn't take bribes from drug dealers. He tries to put the really bad guys behind bars. So he pockets loose money here and there. I accept him for what he is."

"What will you do?"

"I don't know. Locating the Bandelier pot is a long shot at best. Without Fletcher's help, it may be impossible. Maybe there was something on Guvelly's body or in his room that would put me on the trail."

"What would you do with the Bandelier pot if you found it?"

"Turn it over to Fletcher so he could turn it in and we could split the finder's fee."

"Or you could give it to those two thugs from firstNAtions and avoid being beaten to death."

"Or that," I agreed.

20

Tristan arrived the next morning bearing a laptop computer, a miniature camera, another device I didn't recognize and two lattes. At least it was morning by his standards—about forty-five minutes after noon.

The lattes were in brown paper cups and wrapped in waffled cardboard sleeves designed so that you can lift them to your lips without incurring first-degree burns.

"That's six bucks' worth of coffee," I said. "A little extravagant, don't you think?"

"You don't expect me to drink that stuff you brew for your customers, do you? Especially after it's been sitting there all morning."

He had a point. I took a sip of the latte and immediately wanted a biscotti. Or is the singular biscotto?

Tristan opened the laptop, connected it to the laser device, punched a few keys and then asked me if I had come home at 6:57 Friday morning. I told him it had been late Thursday midnight, and he informed me that someone had crossed my threshold at 6:57.

"When did they leave?"

"The next signal break was recorded at 9:22 that same morning."

"That was Reggie coming in to check on me. Nothing between 6:57 and 9:22?"

"Nope."

"So if a prowler entered early that morning, how did he get out without his leaving time being recorded? He obviously wasn't here when Reggie came in."

"The time is recorded when the beam is interrupted. I guess he stepped over it."

"Why would he step over it?"

Tristan thought about it for a few seconds. "He knew there was a beam because he heard the bong sound when he came in. So he stepped over it when he left to avoid making the bong sound again."

"He?"

"I'm assuming it was a he. But next time, you'll know. I'm installing a camera that will be activated when the laser is interrupted. It will take a picture of the doorway and then go back to standby until the next beam interruption."

"I hope there won't be a next time. But even if there is, I don't want a bunch of cables and wires running all over my shop."

"There won't be any. Signals between the laser and the camera will be Bluetooth."

"Bluetooth?"

"It's a frequency-hopping radio link between wireless devices using a protocol—"

"Tristan?"

He looked up from the computer screen sheepishly. "Sorry."

"Just show me what I need to do."

He pointed out an icon of the front door. When you double click it, a report pops up listing the date and time of every bong. By double clicking on one of the times, you get the picture that was made by that bong. Tristan went outside and walked back in, setting off two bongs. I double clicked the icon and got the list he had shown me. It now had two new entries, one at 13:07:51 and the next at 13:07:58. I clicked on the first one and got a picture of Tristan's back. The second one captured his smiling countenance coming through the door.

We placed the camera atop a display case behind a pot where it could see but still be inconspicuous. The computer was placed on a shelf below the counter, but only after I resisted Tristan's sale pitch for something called a point of sale computer that would replace the cash register, check the rubber content of checks before they were accepted, verify credit cards, keep inventory, and so far as I knew, brew the coffee. I pointed out that my entire inventory at that time was ninety-eight pots, each of which was clearly visible from the counter or in one of the cabinets. I could take inventory in less than an hour, and the only digital assistance required was my pointing finger.

Tristan then brought out a satellite radio. I told him I didn't want it, but he made a persuasive argument.

"It used to be that every time I came here you were listening to music, Count Ellington, Duke Basie, that old stuff you like."

"That's Count Basie and Duke Ellington."

"Whatever," he replied. Then he seemed to be in thought for a few seconds. "Which ranks higher," he asked, "a count or a duke?"

"I think it's a—"

"Well," he continued, "there's no music playing now, and there hasn't been the last few times I was here."

"My cassette player is broken."

"Toss it. It's old technology. Even if you wanted to get it fixed, no one works on those anymore."

"So what am I supposed to do with my cassette collection?"

"Toss those too. They already sound bad, and in a few years the magnetized oxide on them will lose whatever feeble music it still possesses. And you don't have to buy CDs. You can get everything on this radio without having to keep any collection in any format."

"You know I don't like the music they play on the radio."

"You used to like NPR."

"Sometimes," I admitted. "At least they had some programs that played the old standards. But they've pretty much sold out in order to compete with commercial radio."

"Really?"

"Just because they're non-profit doesn't mean they don't chase the dollar like everyone else."

"Yeah. Every time I tune in they're doing a pledge drive."

"Taking donations is one thing," I said. "Selling ads is another."

"They don't sell ads, Uncle Hubert."

"Maybe they don't call them ads, but have you listened to their listing of sponsors? It started off innocently enough. They used to say something like 'The following program underwritten by Exxon.' Then they started adding tag lines like 'The following program underwritten by Exxon, a global energy company.' Now they've lifted all restrictions, and you hear things like 'The following program underwritten by Exxon, a global energy company protecting the environment while bringing products to you that heat your home, fuel your car and make life better through petrochemical research and innovation.' Sounds like an ad to me."

"I see what you mean. And they play classical rather than what you like."

"Classical is bad enough, but now they even have call-in shows. Talk radio on NPR! My tax dollars supporting a show where any idiot with a dime can subject me to his analysis of free trade or the Middle East peace process. What's next? Reality radio where a dozen listeners are stranded on an island and have to fight over whether to hear Wagner or Beethoven?"

"Uncle Hubert?"

"Yes."

"Is this still about why you don't want satellite radio?"

"I went off on a tangent, didn't I?"

He nodded. "Satellite radio has channels that play the kind of music you like twenty-four hours a day."

"Really?"

He nodded again.

"You can leave it here, but I doubt if I'll use it."

I asked Tristan how much I owed him for the camera, the laptop and the radio. He waved off the question.

"Let's call the radio a loaner until we see if you like it. The laptop is a relic I stopped using months ago, and digital cameras have been commoditized. They cost next to nothing."

"Commoditized? That's a word?"

He ignored my question and said, "Selena Wright invited me to the alternative band concert next week, so I may need a little help."

"What are these bands alternative to—music?"

He laughed his rumbly laugh. "You would probably think so."

I extracted two hundred dollars from my old-fashioned cash register and passed the bills to him. He seemed genuinely pleased.

I checked my new laptop after he left and, sure enough, there was a snap of him crossing the threshold on his way out. Even frozen in a picture, I could recognize his loping gait that makes me think he must be whistling when he walks.

21

I walked over to the Church after Tristan left. Father Groaz was hearing confessions, but the line was short and the people in it didn't look like major sinners. I decided to wait.

The current San Felipe de Neri Church is new by Old Town standards. It was built in 1793 to replace the previous one built in 1706. It's a beautiful building, somehow managing to combine quaint and majestic with its sloping adobe walls and Victorian details that were obviously added later. The inside is equally appealing, with a stamped metal ceiling and an altar and walls that look like marble but are in fact just your *oeil* being *tromped* by a clever paint job.

Neri has been an active parish for three centuries, so I guess it's had scores of priests. How Groaz was assigned there must be a Holy Mystery. He does look like he belongs out West. With his barrel chest and bushy beard, he could pass for Grizzly Adams. But when he talks, he sounds like Béla Lugosi in those old vampire movies.

I took a seat in a pew with a view of the confessional. Murmured conversation hung in air that was cool and still with the must of old wood and incense. Swales had been worn into the aisles by the shoes of twelve generations of worshippers. A few unadorned electrical fixtures looked like afterthoughts, their small bulbs straining unsuccessfully to light the altar and high ceiling. Only the sunlight streaming through the stained glass gave any life to the sanctuary.

The last sinner left, presumably forgiven, and Groaz emerged moments later.

"Well, Hubert," he started, but it sounded like "Woll, Youbird."

He asked if I had come for confession.

"I'm not Catholic, Father."

"I know that, Youbird, bot someone must do penance for sending that girl to me."

"Where is she?"

"I put her with one of our teachers in the parish school, bot she hazz run away."

"Susannah warned me she might do that."

"How did she know this?"

"She said Kaylee can relate to men only through sex, so she would continue to seek someone who she thought she could attach herself to by offering sex."

"Susannah is vahry perspicacious," he said. Then he lowered his voice and said, "Kaylee attempt to seduce me."

"Jesus Christ!"

"Is exactly whot I said, Youbird, but in a more reverent voice."

"Sorry, Father."

"Is okay. I am a priest and not a handsome man, but is not the first time a woman try to tempt me. It is nothing about me. They seek help, but don't know how to find it. Now she is gone, so we cannot help her."

"Hmm. I'm not so sure."

I walked back around the corner to my shop half expecting to find Kaylee there, but I found Reggie West instead.

"I saw you coming around the corner and thought I'd come say hello. My business is almost as slow as yours."

"Thanks a lot."

"If you're going to make a pot," he said, "I wouldn't mind watching. I'm not likely to sell any gelato today, and I'm intrigued by your work." He had a big curved smile under his perfectly level flattop.

I didn't believe he had any interest in seeing me work. I figured he was bored or just wanted me to listen to more complaints about the alimony.

"Actually," I told him, "my nephew brought me a satellite radio, and I'm going to see if I can figure out how to operate it."

"Maybe another time," he said.

There was an awkward moment while we both stood silent. Then we said our goodbyes and he left.

I started to read the manual that came with the satellite radio. It made the Pythagoras anthology seem like a John Grisham thriller. Finally I gave up and just plugged the thing in.

The plug was the only feature the device shared with any radio I had owned in the past. It had the standard little prongs attached to a cord that was too short to reach an outlet from anyplace you were likely to want a radio. The only thing I can figure is the companies that manufacture electrical appliances are also the ones that make extension cords.

I didn't have an extension cord that wasn't in use, so I pushed my easy chair next to an outlet and held the radio in my lap. There were no knobs, only buttons. And not a single word anywhere. Only symbols. When did all this change? Why did it change? What was wrong with a knob with *Volume* printed under it? At least you knew if you turned the thing, the music would get louder. Now we get hieroglyphics. I can read the ones left by the Anasazi but not the ones on my new radio.

I realized I was working myself into a snit, so I poured myself a glass of Gruet and told myself to relax. I eased back into the chair, sipped the champagne and looked at the buttons. One had a nearly closed circle with a line sticking out through the open part of the circle. The laptop had that symbol on the button that turns it on. I punched it and music started playing. The circle and line thing must be the new hieroglyphic for *On*.

It was on a station playing what I think they call soft rock, an oxymoron if ever there were one. There were two buttons next to the On button, one with a little arrow pointing up and another with a little arrow pointing down. I pushed the Up button and a different channel came on. I pushed the Down button and the soft rock came back. This is too easy, I thought to myself, and took another sip of champagne.

Then I started pushing the Up button and discovering there are more varieties of music than I ever imagined. I stopped on a station with music that seemed to be created with instruments like wind chimes, bamboo sticks and trickling water. Above all that a single plucked string seemed off key but in a pleasant way. The music had an Asian feel to it, and I decided to leave that station on, partly because I was intrigued by the music and partly because I was tired of pushing the button.

Then I fell asleep. When I awoke the same sort of music was playing. Sometimes technology is good. When I got up the energy to push the button again, I thought to myself, I might eventually work my way up to the music I really like.

22

I was feeling good about Tristan's visit and my newfound mastery of technology until I stepped inside Dos Hermanas and saw Sven Nordquist, *nee* Steven Nordquist, standing at the bar. I tried to turn so he wouldn't see me but failed.

"Hello, Hubert."

"Steve," I said, keeping my voice neutral.

Sven is tall and thin with blond hair and eyes as cold as an arctic fjord. His peculiar gait, rigid from his hips to his neck but loose of arm, makes him appear effeminate.

He aimed those cobalt eyes at me. "I go by Sven now."

I nodded. His cologne smelled of fresh berries. He wore an expensive understated suit with a lapel pin that said *ARRIS* on a crest of feathers.

Steve and I were students together. UNM has a good anthropology department, so I never understood how he achieved admission. Despite devoting long hours to the attempt, he was unable to grasp the simplest basics of the subject. He couldn't distinguish *sinanthropus pekinensis* from Piltdown man. Or from a French poodle for that matter. But there was an intensity about him, the kind of single-mindedness that one might associate with success as a student. Yet despite his unbending work ethic, he never mastered the topic, eventually abandoning the science of anthropology for the pseudo-science of "ethnic studies" in which received a master's degree with honors.

"It's been a long time," he said in his flat Midwestern accent.

"Since what?"

"Since we've seen each other."

"You didn't come here to see me, did you?"

"No, I'm waiting for a donor."

"An organ donor? Which one do you need?"

"Same old Hubert," he said without humor. "I'm meeting someone who supports the Alliance for Reconciliation and Repatriation of Indigenous Societies."

"Which I understand goes by the acronym ARRIS."

"As executive director, I'm sure my membership will be happy to hear that you know that," he said.

In fact, I knew it only because of the lapel pin.

"What does it mean?" I asked.

"It means our campaign to establish credibility is succeeding."

"No. I meant what does ARRIS mean? No one selects a name like that unless the letters mean something."

"In woodworking, an arris is the edge where two surfaces meet."

He smiled broadly showing perfect white teeth. The turquoise bracelet he wore seemed out of place with the suit. Or, given that we were in Albuquerque, I guess it was the suit that seemed out of place with the bracelet.

"The two surfaces in this case being Native Americans and whites," I guessed.

"Precisely. We believe the future of our planet lies in that interface."

"Holy interstices!"

He gave me his indulgent smile.

"I think you know our aims," he said.

"Would this be a fair summary? You want the descendants of the Europeans who seized the Americas to give it back to the native peoples. You want those of us who are not native peoples to adopt the culture of the native peoples so that we can remain here with them and live in peace."

"An oversimplification, but basically correct. We believe in reconciliation."

"So do I win the all expenses paid trip to Machu Picchu?"

"What would you do there, steal more pots?"

I feigned hurt. "That doesn't sound very conciliatory. And just to set the record straight, I've never stolen anything."

"You forget I was there at Gran Quivira."

"Well, I try to."

"You are worse than a common thief, Hubert. You don't just steal objects. You steal patrimony."

"Patrimony is a rather Eurocentric term for the executive director of ARRIS to be using."

He lifted his chin which emphasized how much taller he is than me. "We at ARRIS are above petty disputes. We know the traditional ways of the indigenous societies of the western hemisphere resonate with Mother Earth, and whites can be brought to understand this. We believe you and other whites will see the damage your culture is doing to our environment, and when you begin to despair of finding scientific solutions to global issues like pollution and climate change, you will be ready to peacefully lay aside your linear, mathematical, hyper-rationalized weltanschauung."

"Wow. From which native language did you borrow the word *weltanschauung*?"

"You're a clever guy, Hubert, but I am too strong to be provoked. I ask only that you remember that just as a laying down of arms can bring physical peace, so too can a laying down of European culture bring spiritual peace and harmony with nature."

"Do you get paid overtime for the hours you spend memorizing this gibberish?"

He shook his head as if I were a recalcitrant student. Fortunately, Susannah arrived and I escaped Sven's company.

23

"Who's the handsome guy in the expensive suit?"

"He was Steven Nordquist when I first met him, but he changed his name to Sven. He's a professional do-gooder working for what he considers the interests of Native Americans. I won't tell Kauffmann you think he's handsome."

"Why did he change his name to Sven?"

"It was an act of solidarity with oppressed people."

She did that twisty thing with her shoulders and neck and said, "I don't get it. How many Indians are named Sven?"

"It was when he was still in Wisconsin, before he took up the cause of the Indians. The oppressed people he was concerned about back then were Norwegians."

"Norwegians are an oppressed people?"

"Shocking, isn't it?"

"Who oppressed them?"

"I think it was the Danes. Or maybe the Swedes. I'm a little fuzzy on my Scandinavian history."

"Is 'Schuze' a Scandinavian name?"

"Not so far as I know."

"Too bad, 'Nordquist and Schuze' would be a great name for a company, maybe a department store."

"And what sort of store would you start under your name?"

"Susannah's Dating Service?"

"I meant your last name."

"Inchaustiqui's Shepherd Service. What else would you do with a Basque name?"

The sylphlike Angie appeared unbeckoned with our drinks, chips, and salsa.

I told Susannah about ARRIS.

"Is ARRIS like firstNAtions?"

"I don't know anything about firstNAtions, so I can't say."

"Judging from those two who came to your shop, I think first-NAtions must be more like the American Indian Movement."

I hadn't thought about AIM for years, and I found myself wondering what happened to them.

"You're too young to remember AIM," I said.

"I don't have to remember. We learned about them in minority politics."

"That's when you were majoring in political science?"

"Actually, it was pre-law." She shivered. "I can't believe I wanted to be a lawyer."

I was dredging up a few old memories about AIM. I remembered one in particular and asked her if she knew that AIM painted Plymouth Rock red.

"Why did they do that?"

"I guess Plymouth Rock is a symbol of the European invasion."

She turned her palms up and rolled her eyes. "Geez, I know that, Hubie. I meant why red?"

"Well, the first thing that comes to mind is probably not right."

"You mean redskins?"

"So you thought that too?"

"I did, but I didn't want to say it."

"Maybe the red symbolized the blood of all the Indians who were killed," she ventured.

"Maybe. But most of them died from diseases that came with the Europeans."

"You don't believe that story that the Europeans gave the Indians small pox on purpose, do you?"

"The Europeans of the 15th century didn't know any more about the transmission of viruses than the Indians did. It was just bad luck."

"But why did it kill the Indians and not the Europeans."

"Millions of Europeans *did* die from it. They contracted it from the cows and chickens that lived in their houses, but over the centuries, they eventually developed some degree of immunity."

"So the Indians weren't immune because they didn't live with animals?"

I nodded.

"That doesn't seem fair. People who are crazy enough to bed down with livestock should be the ones who get sick. Do you think groups like AIM, ARRIS and firstNAtions do any good?"

"Probably. At least they advocate for people who have been marginalized, and maybe they generate a little hope and self-respect. I remember after AIM occupied Alcatraz, federal funding for the BIA increased. They say you have to make noise to be heard. Of course their larger visions are wildly quixotic."

"Like wanting European culture to disappear."

"Yeah. That rhetoric seems ridiculous to us, but I guess if you're totally downtrodden, it sounds like a beautiful dream."

"So why would someone who voluntarily takes the name Sven want European culture to disappear?"

"That's one downside of groups like ARRIS. They attract a lot of cranks. I suspect Sven is just working out his guilt at being white. ARRIS believes, to quote Sven, that, 'the traditional ways of the indigenous societies of the western hemisphere resonate with Mother Earth, and whites can be brought to understand this.'"

"And he wants to lead us out of whiteness."

"I think that's the program."

"Did you know him well in school?"

"Not really."

"But the way you described your conversation just now, it sounded sort of hostile."

"He still seems to have a lot of hostility towards me. I don't like him because he's supercilious and self righteous, but I wouldn't waste any of my limited store of hostility on him."

"Why is he hostile toward you?"

"I think it's because he's the one who reported me for selling pots and got me kicked out of school."

"I don't get it. That sounds like a reason for you to be hostile to him, not the other way around."

"Then this is a perfect place to insert my philosophy that he who harms another suffers more damage than the one he harms."

"You made that up?"

"Actually, I heard it on an old television show called Kung Fu when I was in high school.

"Black and white?"

I just gave her a look.

"Just kidding," she said. "So you think Sven is hostile towards you because he sort of feels guilty about harming you?"

"Maybe. The irony is that he didn't harm me. All he did was report the truth to the department head. And if I hadn't been kicked out of school, I wouldn't have my shop."

"And we wouldn't be sitting here drinking margaritas."

"Right."

"So," she said, lifting her glass, "here's to Sven."

"I'll drink to that."

24

Susannah left for class, and I sat at our table deciding what to do about dinner. Across the way, I saw Sven depart, his torso moving along as if on rails while his limber arms swung rhythmically.

His intended victim I recognized as Farley Ezekiel, whom I knew well by reputation as a benefactor and not well personally because he had been introduced to me only once and briefly by Layton Kent. To my surprise, he recognized me and stopped by my table on his way out.

"Hubert Schuze, am I correct?"

"I'm impressed, Mr. Ezekiel."

He gave a hearty laugh. "Don't be. My memory grows worse with each passing day. But it pays to remember people introduced by Layton Kent."

"I assure you my connection with Mr. Kent is quite tenuous. Can I buy you dinner?"

"Will it involve a solicitation for a gift?"

"It will not."

"Then I accept."

Angie appeared the instant Farley sat down, and she took our orders. *Tamales* for me and *Sopa de Lima* for him.

The conversation eventually turned to his meeting with Sven.

"I gather you two know each other," he said. "Is he a close friend?"

"Our chance encounter here was the first time I've seen him in perhaps five years."

"Lucky you," he said and then quickly added, "That was unkind. The fellow seems so committed. But also desperate. As you perhaps know, I contribute to a number of causes I deem worthy, but I never give based on desperation. I gave a small token when ARRIS was founded—call it seed money—and I was willing to give more had he convinced me that ARRIS was doing something worthwhile. But his pitch tonight was that they needed funding to avoid going under. Who gives money merely to keep an organization afloat?"

I felt a twinge of sympathy for Sven. I can sell one small pot a month and clear fifty thousand a year, but poor Sven has to beg and scrape just to make ends meet. Given what an ass he is, I should have felt good, but I felt sad instead.

As I walked among the adobe buildings on the way back to my shop, I felt better. In fact, I felt great. The moon was just rising above the bell tower of San Felipe, and the air was scented with piñon.

And there in front of my shop was Kaylee.

"Hi, Hubert."

I unlocked the door. "Come inside," I said brusquely.

"Hubert, I—"

"Don't say anything."

She followed me back to my living quarters where I picked up the phone and called Tristan.

"Hi, Uncle Hubert."

It always unnerves me that he knows it's me before I say anything.

"I've got a young lady here who came to Albuquerque a week ago with just the clothes on her back. She needs a place to stay."

"Is she a runaway?"

"Yes."

"How old is she?"

"Right."

"She's standing there and you can't talk?"

"Exactly."

"Is she younger or older than me?"

"About the same."

"Is she messed up somehow?"

"I think so."

"Drugs."

"I don't think so."

"Abused?"

"Possibly."

"Hold on a minute."

He came back on the line a few minutes later and said his neighbor, a graduate student at the University, was willing to put her up for a day or two if that would help.

"Is your neighbor a man or a woman?"

"A woman."

"Good."

"The girl's afraid of men right now?"

"Quite the opposite."

"That's why you don't want her there?"

"Exactly."

"So will she make a pass at me?"

"No doubt, but then most young women do."

He laughed. "I wouldn't say most."

"This sort of goes beyond—"

"She grabs at anything in pants?"

"She was at the Church temporarily."

He hesitated at my apparent *non-sequitor*. "Is that important?"

"It's related to what we were just talking about."

He was silent for a moment. "Are you saying she made a pass at Father Groaz?"

"Yes."

"I'll come get her. And I'll warn Emily."

I hung up and turned to Kaylee. "My nephew is coming to get you. He has a place where you can stay. If you run off again, I'm not going to have anything more to do with you. If you come back, I'll just call the police and they can turn you over to social services. Do you understand that?"

She frowned and nodded.

25

"I don't know much about them, but from what I've heard, you don't want to mess with these guys, round eyes."

Martin Seepu handed the firstNAtions card back to me.

"Thank you, Tonto," I said. "Can you be a little more specific?"

"Are you going to buy the pot?" Martin asked.

"You won't answer my question unless I buy the pot?"

"Right."

"That's blackmail."

"Right."

"Fair enough. I'll buy it."

"You want to know the price?" he asked.

"I assume it's the usual, twenty-four dollars' worth of beads?"

"You want Manhattan, that's a fair price. But the pot is two thousand."

"I won't pay more than twenty-five hundred."

"White devil drive-hard bargain. Two thousand for my uncle and five hundred for the scholarship fund?"

I nodded and counted out twenty-five pictures of Ben Franklin. Martin rolled them up and stuffed them in his jeans.

"I'll ask around about firstNAtions," he said.

"Thanks. How old is the pot?"

"I don't know. Thirty, maybe fifty years. The old man can remember everything that ever happened in his life. He just can't remember when."

Martin was wearing jeans that looked like they'd survived a few too many rodeos and a Western pearl-buttoned shirt with the sleeves rolled up above his elbows. He's ten years younger than me. He's no taller than me but outweighs me by thirty pounds, all of it muscle. The shirt fit him like a second skin.

Martin's pueblo is nine miles from town. His uncle is a gifted potter who would be wealthy if he sold more pots. But he only let's Martin bring me one when he wants a little cash, which is usually only two or three times a year.

"Same terms as always," I said. "If he decides he wants this one back, let me know. If I haven't sold it, you can have it back for what I paid for it."

Martin poured himself some coffee. He took a sip and shuddered. "Bad enough you had to steal our land."

"I can't seem get the hang of it."

"It's the water, Kemo Sabe. You draw this from the Rio Grande?"

"No, right from the tap."

"In Albuquerque, that's almost the same thing. In the Pueblo, we get our water from a spring. It's pure and sweet."

"Makes good coffee?"

He looked at me over the rim of his cup. "I'll bring you some."

26

After Martin left, I polished his uncle's pot with a soft rag and granted it pride of place on a display shelf close to the counter where I could look at it. It had the cloud and lightning motif peculiar to Martin's pueblo. Each stylized cloud had a zigzag bolt descending at an angle toward the ground.

I wondered how Martin's uncle spaced the patterns. It's easy for me because I have something to copy. But Native American potters do not create standard-sized pots. Their wares are made at home by hand, not in a factory by machines. If they make ten pots like the one I was looking at, there might be ten different circumferences varying by half an inch or so. And yet the background space between each design motif is invariably uniform.

The more I thought about it, the more it puzzled me. I took the pot back to my workshop and sat down where thinking about pot-making comes naturally—at my wheel.

If I wanted to copy the pot, I'd just measure the circumference and the distance between the symbols and copy them. But what if I weren't making a copy? What if I were starting from scratch?

I removed the plastic wrap from some clay I'd dug from the bed of the Rio Puerco and kneaded it into a ball. I started the wheel and pushed my thumbs into the ball, gradually exerting pressure until I had a simple pot. Then I used the parentheses formed by my thumbs and pointing fingers to make the pot symmetrical as it turned, my hand exerting gentle pressure until there were no high or low spots. You develop a feel for that over the years.

I turned off the wheel and watched it spin to a stop. I liked the form I'd created and wondered briefly if I should try to make pots of my own design. I'd tried it in the past and never liked the result, so I let the thought slip and stared at the pot.

How would I place a series of designs around it? I picked up a clay knife and laid it gently across the top of my glistening new pot. The knife made indentions on opposite sides of the rim. I rotated the wheel ninety degrees and repeated the process so that I now had four evenly spaced indentions.

Big deal. It's easy to get even spacing if the number of designs is a power of two. But the pot from Martin's uncle had seventeen clouds around its perimeter. How do you get equal spacing in that case?

You could measure the circumference and divide by seventeen. Martin's uncle could do that. I could do that. But a Mogollon potter could not have done that. They had no measuring tapes. They had no system of exact measurement. Their counting system very likely had no numbers higher than ten. Yet they managed to get perfect spacing on their pots.

I decided to see if I could work out some way of achieving that spacing using only things the Mogollon had at their disposal. They didn't have measuring tapes, but they could have had a straightedge and a compass. Pythagoras demonstrated that you can do a lot of geometry with just those two implements. I had a straightedge in the form of my clay knife. I rifled around my toolbox until I found a compass. No, not the thing that points north. This was the hinged thing with a point on one leg and a pencil on the other. It's the thing people forget about after their geometry class right after they forget about hypotenuses. Or are they hypoteni?

The Mogollon could have had both. Their compass wouldn't have looked like ours, of course. It might have been a forked stick with one end dipped in the ashes of last night's fire so it could make a mark on the clay.

You can create a right angle using only a straightedge and a compass. If you can create a right angle, you can create a right triangle, and you can use Pythagoras' theorem to find the lengths of the sides. Of course Mogollon teenagers were spared learning the famous formula, so they wouldn't have done it that way.

However, they did know about triangles. They decorated their pots with them, and they might have used another Pythagorean method involving isomorphic triangles. The idea is to lay out the number of . . . Well, I'm probably telling you more than you want to know, and it doesn't matter because at this point I looked out on the street and saw Susannah with a paper cup in each hand. I was surprised because I usually don't see her during the day. She walked up to my shop and kicked the door. I opened it.

"This is an intervention," she said. She placed the coffees on a shelf full of clay and then walked back and locked the door. When she came back to the workshop, she frowned at my new pot with slits in the rim and the straightedge and compass.

I explained what I was trying to do.

"Suppose you figure out how they did it," she asked. "What good will it do?"

"It will satisfy my curiosity."

"No offense, Hubie, but does it ever occur to you that you might spend the same amount of energy and solve a practical problem?"

"I don't think you can always distinguish between practical and impractical. Some of the world's most important practical problems were solved using discoveries made by people who were just following their curiosity with no particular application in mind."

"Yeah? Like what?"

"Well, about seventy years ago, a scientist was tinkering with high-frequency radar waves just out of curiosity and he noticed a candy bar in his pocket had softened. And that's how he discovered the microwave oven."

She shrugged. "Have you gotten anywhere?"

"I don't know. I was hoping I could use isomorphic triangles to divide the circumference of a pot into equal segments."

"I don't know what isomorphic means in triangles, but in drawing it's a way of representing three-dimensional objects without using normal perspective," she said.

I began, "Isomorphic triangles are—"

"I came here to intervene. I'm not interested in geometry right now."

"Oh."

"Is that true about the microwave?"

I told her it was and she handed me my coffee. "Look at the logo on that cup," she said after I took a sip.

I looked. Then she handed me a card from her employer, La Placita.

"Look at that logo."

I looked again.

"What you need," she said, "is a logo."

"I don't know, Suze. I've operated all these years without—"

"A name," she interjected. She shook her head in exasperation. "You've operated all these years without even a name. So before we get you a logo, you have to choose a name."

"I can't choose. That's why I don't have one. I tried to find one for about a month when I first opened. I spent hours on it, but nothing I could think of was ever quite right. Then at the end of the first month, I was doing my bookkeeping and realized I had done surprisingly well. The problem was my shrinking inventory. So if I was going to stay in business, I had to start replacing the pots I was selling. I spent some time digging, some scouting the pueblos and some placing and answering ads offering to buy old Indian pots. Between inventory building and shop tending, I didn't have time to think up a name, so I just let it slide. My business grew steadily. After a few months I realized that not having an official name wasn't keeping me from making money. So I just stopped thinking about it."

"But how do you advertise?"

"I'm in the yellow pages under several categories—Pottery, Native American Merchandise, Curios, Antiques and Specialty Shops."

"But what do the ads *say?*"

"They all say the same thing: 'Classic Native American pottery bought, sold, and traded.' Then they give my phone number and address."

"An ad without a business name?"

I shrugged.

"How do they know where to put you in the list of stores in each category?"

"The list me alphabetically under *C*."

"*C*?"

"Right. C for 'Classic Native American pottery bought, sold—'"

"Geez, this is hopeless. Look, Hubie, I have some fellow students in one of my art history courses. They're studio students, but they take art history as a related minor. In one of their studio courses, a design seminar, they have to do a group project, and they want to design a logo."

"They don't need my help to do that."

"They do. They could make one up for an imaginary business. But if the project is real life, if a business actually uses their logo, they'll almost certainly get a better grade. And it will look great on their résumés that they had a real live client and produced satisfactory work."

"What if the work isn't satisfactory?"

"Then you won't have to use it."

"Hmm."

"You'll do it, won't you?"

"I guess so," I mumbled.

"This is so great. They're very talented. You won't be disappointed. Now we need the name you want to use."

"I've already told you I couldn't pick a name. Let's just leave it at the logo."

"How can you design a logo without knowing the name of the business?"

"Okay, how about 'Pot Thieves ⊠ Us'?"

"Very funny."

"Pilfered Pottery?"

She just shook her head.

"Okay, I'll make you a deal. You have them design a logo. They know what I do. Well, some of what I do. You can even bring them by to see the shop and the pots. When I see their design, I'll try to pick a name that fits the design."

"That's a great idea. I can see it on their résumés: 'Designed a logo for a client who was so pleased that he named his business based on it.' It's almost like what we were talking about earlier, isomorphic drawing."

I felt my brow furrow. "How is it like isomorphic drawing?"

"Because you're moving from the logo to the name instead of the other way around."

Now I was even more confused. "You mean isomorphic drawings are backwards?"

"Not backwards, exactly. They go from something with perspective to the same thing without perspective, so it's sort of the reverse of the normal 3-D drawing."

"I don't get it."

"Look, suppose you draw a cube. If you look straight at it and draw what you see, the drawing will be a square, right?"

"Right, because you see only one side."

"But if you want to show it's a cube instead of just a square, you could draw it from an angle, say above and to the left. Then you could see three sides, or maybe I should say two sides and the top."

I nodded in understanding.

"But when you look at a cube from that angle, you have to add perspective. The three surfaces you draw will not be squares like the side you drew when you were looking straight at the cube. The front will still be a square, but the side and the top will be parallelograms."

She made a sketch to illustrate.

"If you want to show a 3-D image without the distortion of normal perspective, that is, without using a vanishing point, then you can make an isometric drawing." She drew a big rectangle on one side of the paper. "Say this is your frame. You draw the perspective cube outside the frame. Then you connect the corner points back inside like this." And she drew some lines.

And I sat there staring at a design outside of the frame connected to a similar but still different one inside. And I stared at it some more.

"Susannah, you're a genius!"

"Because I can explain isomorphic drawing?"

"That, too. But mainly because you just gave me the perfect example of how idle curiosity can lead to the solution of a very practical problem."

Although I didn't tell Susannah at that point, the practical problem solved in this case was how to get the pot out of the Valle del Rio Museum. And just as I had expected, it came about while I was thinking about math and trying to see things from a fresh perspective.

Okay, the solution didn't *really* arise directly from trying to solve the spacing problem geometrically. It actually came about because of Susannah's drawing, but that drawing was a new perspective, and that's what's needed to solve problems that look like they have no solution.

27

Saturday had broken clear and crisp, and the plan I had discovered for getting the pot from the Museum made the day seem even brighter.

I drove south toward the Isleta Pueblo until I reached the unnamed dirt road that leads to the residence of Emilio and Consuela Sanchez.

"Bienvenido, Señor Uberto."

"Buenos días, Señor Sanchez."

"Consuela, she is in the kitchen."

"That is good news for both of us, *amigo*."

I put a hand on his shoulder and stopped him before we went in. "How is she doing?"

"She looks to me the same as always, but perhaps that is because we grow old together."

She was peeling freshly roasted chilies on a counter laden with enough vessels of food to supply a wagon train.

"You've been roasting poblanos, Señora Sanchez."

"What do I say, Emilio? Uberto has the nose for every chili. But you must call me Consuela."

We chatted for an hour about what she was planning to grow in the garden that spring, and she asked if she could plant something for me. I told her chilies, preferably poblanos.

"You always ask for chilies. What else would you like?"

"Fresh oregano."

"Is always the same, chilies and oregano."

"The recipes are the same, so the ingredients must be the same."

"Those recipes I brought with me from Chihuahua as a girl. Now they are old and tired like me."

"They are not old. They are classic. And judging from this kitchen, you are not tired."

"It is messy, no?"

"It is a place where a cook is working." I had a brainstorm. "You should publish a cookbook with your recipes and traditional techniques of the Northern Mexican kitchen."

She laughed out loud.

"Consuela, Uberto gives us a good idea. You are the best cook of traditional Mexican food. Such a book would be a good thing."

She picked up a large knife and playfully waved it at both of us. "You two are like small boys. Now sit down for the food and say no more about cookbooks."

She made her corn and poblano soup. In one pan, she sautés chopped onions, poblano peppers, garlic and cumin. In a separate pan she uses a big knife to slice the kernels off ears of fresh corn into hot lard and then stirs like crazy until the corn softens. Then she combines the contents of the two pans in a large stockpot, adds chicken broth and lime juice and lets it simmer. When all the flavors have combined, she takes the pot off the heat, throws in fresh oregano and *crema Mexicana* and lets it sit two or three minutes before ladling it into bowls. She serves it with warm corn tortillas and cucumbers slices sprinkled with chili powder and *pilon* sugar.

Emilio and I both had four bowls of it and Consuela beamed with each refill.

28

"Get out of town."

That was me talking to myself. And I meant it. I wanted to escape prowlers, thugs, cops and zealots. Those would be, in order, the mystery intruders who crossed my threshold at 6:57, the two heavies from firstNAtions, Whit Fletcher and Sven Nordquist.

But mainly what I had to do was dig. The plan Susannah had unknowingly inspired to spirit the pot away from the Museum required a special pottery shard, and you can't pick those up at your local Ace Hardware. So I had to get out of town. Back to Gran Quivira. Back to the scene of the crime, so to speak.

So after a relaxing Sunday in my workshop with my hands in clay, I had a delicious dinner of *pollo en mole* and went to bed at the crack of dark. I set the alarm for midnight.

I hate alarm clocks. We would be healthier if we slept until nature woke us in a manner that is, well, natural. Schuze's Anthropology Premise number eight is that schedules are incompatible with the evolutionary history of humans. Americans and northern Europeans love schedules. We're dismayed by cultures that don't follow them. We joke about Mexicans saying *mañana* and Jamaicans talking about "island time." But we are the ones who've got it wrong. We spent most of our million-and-a-half-year history living like lions, sleeping when we were tired, hunting when we were hungry and running when we were threatened. These things don't happen on a nine-to-five schedule. Pots weren't made on an assembly line. We made one when we needed one.

Although it is rarely set, I do own an alarm clock. A special one. When the wake-up time arrives, a chime sounds ever so softly. Moments later, it chimes again with only a slight surge in decibels. These incremental increases in volume continue until you become gradually aware of the chimes and wake up slowly as opposed to the rude awakening of a regular alarm. However, when the wake-up time is midnight, even the gentle chime "becomes as sounding brass."

It was bitter cold, so I dressed in a navy blue watch cap and black fleece workout suit over insulated long johns. I loaded the long piece of rebar I use for probing and the two shovels I use for digging and set off in the 1985 Bronco I refer to fondly as my rust bucket.

If you want to visit Gran Quivira, and not many people do, you would normally take State Highway 55 south from the picturesque town of Mountainair. Or you could take Highway 55 north from the town of Claunch, which is about as picturesque as its name suggests. That's what *you* would do because you wouldn't mind driving in right through the main entrance and past the ranger quarters.

I, on the other hand, desired to enter and leave undetected, so I took Interstate 40 east from Albuquerque to Moriarty where I turned south. I stopped in the middle of the road a few miles south of Willard, no problem at that time of the night, or at most times during the day for that matter.

There is something regal about parking in the middle of a highway as if you owned the road. Of course it wasn't the Via Romana or even Interstate 40. It was a small state road in the middle of nowhere.

Actually, it was on the edge of nowhere. The middle would have been more crowded.

I stood in the road and observed moonbeams bouncing off the reflective white strip between the two narrow lanes. Lean old ranchers in beat-up trucks drive this stretch of road, signaling the occasional colleague going the opposite direction with a nod or a lifting of two fingers off the steering wheel.

I laid a strip of canvas in front of each wheel then drove the Bronco forward slightly. I got out and lifted the canvas strips around the tires, securing them by lacing a cord through the grommets installed for that purpose.

With the tires covered, I turned off both the pavement and the headlights and sat silently until my eyes adjusted to the dark. Then I followed a rancher's sandy road as it skirted the north end of a little portion of the Cibola National Forest, which is cut off from the larger forest of the same name across the Rio Grande. I headed south into the fringes of Gran Quivira.

It was a beautiful still night, the cold, dry air so clear the sky looked like a sequined shawl and the moon like a polished ball of ice hovering just above the dunes. A coyote peered at me from behind a mesquite bush. Fifty yards ahead a jackrabbit stood alert, ready to bolt if the coyote came his direction. The land rose slightly to the north and the distant ridge was crenellated by black triangular pines.

Gran Quivira was founded around AD 800 and had thousands of inhabitants. Unfortunately for those thousands, Coronado came calling in 1539 with diseases against which the natives had no immunity, and most of them died in a series of epidemics. A severe drought in the seventeenth century drove out the few remaining occupants.

During our summer dig in Gran Quivira, we started at dawn and knocked off early because it got so hot. I didn't mind the heat, so I walked for miles in every direction getting to know the land. Driving by, it looks like a dry, featureless plain. But when you explore it on foot, you discover subtle elevation changes, varying rock strata, patterns of plant growth and other aspects of a faceted landscape.

I tried to imagine what life had been like for the last few stragglers desperate to stay in their ancestral home. Where would they go for water? The small arroyos directly around the sprawling pueblo would have turned to powder during the drought. I knew from growing up in the desert that after a rain, arroyos dry up in a pattern starting from the portions farthest from the mountains. The people of the Gran Quivira would have walked toward the mountains. And they would have followed the largest arroyo. I already knew where that one was, so I pulled up a few hundred yards from it and walked the rest of the way guided by a moon so bright I could see my shadow in the sand.

In the early days of the AIDS epidemic, a legislator from some conservative state had attended a conference in San Francisco and later declared, evidently with some pride, that he wore shower caps over his shoes while he was in his hotel room out of fear of catching AIDS. The reason I remembered this bizarre story was that I was walking along with two disposable shower caps over my shoes.

I know I looked like an idiot, but what would have looked even more idiotic would be me in a mug shot. Tracking is a difficult skill, and the sandy soil in the wash would probably be unreadable within hours after the usual New Mexico spring wind blew over it the next afternoon, but I did not wish to take any chances that either my tires or my shoes would be identified.

The ruins of Gran Quivira are protected by the National Park Service, but not very well. They take seriously their mandate to make sure no kid from Iowa leaves the park with an arrowhead in his pocket, but the exposed adobes continue to erode. There are about eight million arrowheads and pieces of worked flint in the ground around Gran Quivira, so it's not like they are scarce. Given the low visitor rate, every kid who wants one could take a piece of flint, and the supply would last until Gran Quivira melts back into the earth from neglect or the sun is extinguished, whichever happens first.

By looking at plant growth patterns and rock strata, you can tell where the course of an arroyo has changed in recent years and where it is hundreds of years old. I found a promising site under an overhang on the inside curve of the arroyo. I began to find artifacts after digging only three feet into the packed sand. There were several V-shaped shards of the kind I needed.

I love the high desert at night. The air is cool, clear, and dry, the only scents wafting from creosote bushes and blooming cactus. Because there is nothing in the air, not even moisture, moonbeams arrive unspoiled. On this particular night, they washed the sand in light because the moon was full. Thanks to that and good night vision, I could sort the shards with ease. I took one that looked just right for my purpose and a couple of spares just in case. Then I put the others back in the earth. Professional archaeologists would have been proud of me. I filled the hole I had made, smoothed the sand,

and departed. Or to paraphrase Khalil Gibran, the digging hand digs and, having dug, moves on.

It's difficult to describe the thrill of finding something a fellow human being made a thousand years ago. Suddenly you are in contact with the ancient past. Yet it remains a mystery. The artifact is the tip of the iceberg. Howard Carter put it more poetically when he explained what it was like to dig up Tut and his treasures: "The shadows move, but the dark is never quite dispersed."

The unearthed pot connects me to its maker, one potter to another. It has nothing to do with ethnicity, an accident of birth we use as an excuse to treat different people differently. For some reason I don't understand, we seem obsessed by our minor differences and blind to our vast commonality.

One of the commonest bonds is clay. Every civilization on every continent since the day we first started using our hands for something other than walking has made things of clay. And even though we have passed out of the agricultural age, through the industrial age, and into the information age, clay remains a staple in human life. From the tiles on our floors to the plates on our tables, we use clay every day. Some of us even make a good living selling clay pots.

In 1996, a nine-thousand-year-old skeleton was discovered along the banks of the Columbia River in Washington. It is a striking find for two reasons. It is among the oldest ever found in North America, and it appears to be Caucasian.

I'm Caucasian, but I feel no kinship with those ancient bones. As an archaeologist, however, I am fascinated by them. What was a Caucasian doing along the Columbia River almost nine thousand years before the Voyage of Columbus? Did the prehistoric Vikings sail to America and trek across the continent? Did Caucasian-like people, perhaps the Ainu of Japan, come across the land bridge that is now under the Bering Strait? Are the Mormons correct that there was a white race in America in prehistoric times?

We may never find out because the Umatilla Tribe sued to have the bones interred on their reservation under the Native American Graves Protection and Repatriation Act. Their view is that any human remains on their land must be of their ancestors.

One of the few certainties in the uncertain world of archaeology is that peoples in all places and all times have moved and migrated—SAP number three. The skeletal remains from Washington are absolutely not the ancestors of the Umatilla. The ancient peoples we call the Mogollon are not the ancestors of today's Pueblo Indians. And if a skeleton is dug up under my adobe in Old Town, it will certainly not be my ancestor.

I walked back to my Bronco, took off my shower caps, took the canvas off my tires when I reached the pavement and retraced my route to Albuquerque. I arrived just as the sun peeked over the Sandia Mountains. I ate three eggs with green chili, four chorizos and two corn tortillas. Wielding a shovel works up the appetite. After washing the dishes, I went out to my patio and climbed into the hammock strung between two cottonwood trees over ground, which I am fairly confident is skeleton-free. I fell instantly and deeply asleep.

I awoke without the aid of any mechanical contrivance. It was late afternoon, just in time to shower, shave, don a pair of chinos and a blue oxford cloth shirt and arrive at Dos Hermanas by five sharp.

29

"How was your weekend?" Susannah asked after we settled in to our little corner of Dos Hermanas.

"Thursday night after you left, Kaylee showed up."

"Let me guess. She was huddled on the ground in front of your door again, and you took her in."

I shrugged and said, "Give me your tired, your poor, your huddled masses yearning to breathe free."

"I told you she'd be back. You can't keep taking her in."

"I didn't. I turned her over to Tristan."

"Oh, great. Even normal girls can't keep their hands off him."

"He can take care of himself. Anyway, he got a neighbor of his, a girl, to take her in temporarily."

"So now what?"

"I have no idea."

"Can't the police handle it?"

"I've threatened her with the police, and it works because she doesn't want them involved. But I doubt there's anything they could do. She's twenty-one. It's not against the law to travel around with no possessions and make passes at men."

"Hmm. You don't think she's a criminal, do you? Maybe that's why she's afraid of the police."

"If she's a criminal, she's very bad at it. She had a little over twelve dollars in her wallet. Can you try to think of something?"

"I'll give it some thought, but I'm not very optimistic."

I told her I'd spent most of Saturday with Consuela and Emilio.

"How is she?"

"I don't know how she is physically, but her spirits are high."

"And Emilio?"

"He's a rock."

"That's probably why her spirits are high. I know she wasn't married when you were growing up. She lived with your parents, so how did she meet Emilio?"

"It was a semi-arranged marriage."

"Meaning their families arranged for them to meet but left it to them to decide?"

"How did you guess?"

"A lot of Basque families do that. When I was growing up, my mom never let a day go by without reminding me that my goal in life was to marry a nice Basque boy."

"Maybe you will."

"Oh, it doesn't matter at this point. When I passed eighteen without being married, she gave up the idea of a Basque son-in-law and said she could settle for anyone who was Catholic. When I passed twenty-one, she opened it up to Christians of any denomination. When I passed twenty-five, she became panicky. I think she would settle at this point for any member of the human race."

The sun had dropped below the buildings across the street and the dry desert air was suddenly cooler. I retrieved my Windbreaker from the back of the chair. As I was putting it on, Martin Seepu came through the door.

"Which one of you is buying?" he asked as he took a seat.

"I just gave you twenty-five-hundred dollars on Friday," I reminded him.

"That was for my Uncle."

"Then let him buy."

"He don't drink."

"So I have to buy because your Uncle who isn't even here doesn't drink?"

"Makes sense to me," said Susannah.

I threw up my hands and caught Angie's attention. "Bring this Indian a beer, but keep a close watch on him. He can't hold his liquor." She rolled her eyes, shook her head and walked away. My ethnic humor is sometimes too subtle for her.

Martin asked me what I had done over the weekend, and instead of rehashing what I'd already told Susannah, I told them both how I had spent most of a night at Gran Quivira.

"So you just walked out into the middle of unmarked desert and dug up what you needed?" asked Susannah.

"You make it sound like a needle in a haystack. The desert isn't unmarked. You just have to know how to read the land."

"Like *feng shui*," said Martin.

"I suppose so," I said. "What does that mean, anyway?"

"'*Feng*' means wind and '*shui*' means water. The two forces that shape the desert."

"But *feng shui* is an Asian concept."

"The Gobi Desert is in Asia."

"But you're in North America."

"And you're supposed to be an anthropologist. You never hear about the land bridge across the Bering Strait?"

Angie brought Martin his cold Tecate in a can. She knows what brand he likes.

"What kind of shard you find?" he asked.

I pulled one out of my pocket and showed it to him. He turned it around in his hand and then gave it back to me.

"Doesn't this bother you?" Susannah asked him.

"You think there's bad magic in that shard?"

"No, of course not. But it's Native American. Isn't it somehow, I don't know, irreverent to dig it up and parade it around?"

Martin put some salsa on a chip and popped it in his mouth. Then he took a sip of beer. "The lady who runs the herbal shop two doors north of here calls herself an Africanist. I saw it on her business card. On the back of the card was a word I didn't know, so I asked her what it meant. She said it was the African word for friendship."

We just stared at him, waiting to see where this was going.

He took another sip of beer. "There's no Native American word for friendship. There's no European word for friendship. There's no Asian word for friendship. I don't know much about Africa, but I don't think the whole continent speaks one language."

More staring. Another sip of beer.

"I'm a Native American because my people were here before the Europeans arrived. The people of Grand Quivira were Native American for the same reason. What we have in common is that we were on the same continent in the same time frame. The Basque and the Estonians have as much in common as we do because they're both on the same continent at the same time." Then he turned to me and said with a gleam in his eyes, "You want to make that one of your Premises, you have my permission."

"The Basque and the Estonians?" said Susannah, eyebrows raised.

"You're Basque. I try to pick examples that hit home."

"You think I'm Estonian?" I asked.

"Probably not. You're too short. I just thought the contrast between the two words was nice, sort of a *haiku* ring to them."

"Jeez," said Susannah, "first *feng shui* and now *haiku*."

"It must be the land bridge thing," I offered.

"You guys think I should have a second round before class? There's enough time."

"What class is it?" Martin and I asked in unison.

"What difference does that make?"

Martin and I looked at each other. He pointed to me, so I said, "Some classes call for less sobriety than others."

"It's a seminar in surrealism."

"Have another round," we said, again in unison.

"Surrealism," I said after Angie brought our drinks, "that's like Dalí's painting of the limp clocks?"

"Yeah. That one's called *The Persistence of Memory*."

"I don't get the title," said Martin.

"I don't either," she said. "Seems like it should be called *Loss of Memory* because we don't remember clocks as being soft. And that would also fit in with the philosophy of the surrealists."

"They had a philosophy?" I asked.

She dropped her shoulders and looked at me like I should know better. "Of course they had a philosophy. We're talking art history, not art appreciation."

"Sorry. So what was their philosophy?"

"Wanting to escape reason and reality. They were fascinated with the power of dreams and the irrational."

"Sounds like a mental hospital," said Martin.

She chuckled and said, "They might even agree with you. Dalí claimed to use self-induced hallucinations when he painted."

"So do some Indian artists," said Martin.

"So the limp clocks are supposed to be an hallucination?" I asked.

"I don't know. He called them 'the camembert of time.' Isn't that a great phrase? Anyway, the surrealists wanted to blur the line between reality and fantasy."

I thought for a moment and said, "I'm going to attempt to blur that line myself, thanks to you." Then I told them my plan for extracting the pot from the Valle del Rio Museum and how Susannah's illustration of an isomorphic drawing had inspired it. She was so excited that she volunteered to help.

"You want to be my accomplice?"

"Absolutely."

I thought about it while I took another sip of my margarita. "You can go to the Museum and take some pictures of the pot and measure it."

"That sounds sort of boring, Hubert, like you're giving the safe part of the plan to the girl and keeping the exciting part yourself."

"Not at all. The measuring part will be risky. You'll have to take down one of the ropes and put the tape snugly against the pot at several different places. If the staff catches you, you'll be in trouble. Of course you won't have damaged anything, so they can hardly charge you with a crime, but they won't be very pleasant and they might throw you out. If they find out who you are and report you to the University, you could join me as an ex-student-in-disgrace."

"You think the art history department would kick me out just for touching a pot in the Museum?"

"Probably not. You could just say you needed the measurements for a paper you wanted to write about the pot. Any reasonable person would see your actions as a minor lapse of judgment. But people in the arts are not always reasonable."

"Yeah, remember the surrealists," said Martin.

"Good point. I just want you to go into this with your eyes wide open."

"You're sweet to worry. But really, this is the most fun I can imagine, and we'll be in on something together." She hesitated then said, "But do you really need me? I don't want to spoil anything."

"I need you for two reasons. First, there's a security camera at the entrance. I was in the Museum recently and I'll have to go in one more time. Maybe it's not a big deal, but when they review the pictures from the camera, I think it's better if I'm not on their film three times. Second, the tape measure you'll be using is the cloth type used in sewing. A steel tape like carpenters use would set off the metal alarm. They look in purses and they sometimes ask patrons to empty their pockets into a little dish before passing through the metal detector. You're a girl, so if you just happen to have a cloth tape, they won't think that's unusual, and you can put it back in your pocket or purse."

"A man could carry a sewing tape."

"Only if he were an art historian."

"That's—"

"Just kidding," I added quickly. "I'm just trying to cover every detail no matter how minor."

"So we're planning a heist. This is so exciting."

"In case anyone asks," said Martin, "I was never here."

30

"This one won't make you drowsy," he said to me.

Usually you can't find anyone to help you, which in this case would have suited me fine. But I had found the world's most attentive pharmacist. He wore a white lab coat with a nametag identifying him as Brian. There were no other customers, and I guess he was bored. I told him I wanted to browse, but he insisted on helping.

"That's not the one I'm looking for," I said.

"You have a specific brand in mind? Why didn't you say so? I can find it in a jiffy."

"I don't remember the brand name."

"Do you remember if it made you drowsy? Because there are two general classes of allergy medicines, drowsy and non-drowsy."

"All I remember is it was a spray."

"We have a few of those down this way." He moved along the aisle. "Not as many as we used to have. Most people prefer tablets." He seemed disappointed I didn't want tablets.

"Do they? Well, I want a spray."

"How about this one? It's particularly good against the pollens we get this time of year."

"No, that's not what it looked like. It was in a plastic bottle."

Actually, I had no idea what sort of allergy spray I was seeking because I've never bought one in my life. But I did know I wanted a plastic spray bottle and one with an allergy spray label on it would suit my purposes well.

I was about to give up and try another store.

"This one?" the clerk said, holding up a spray bottle of the sort I wanted.

"That's the one."

"I don't recommend this brand. It's really just a saline nasal spray to moisten the sinus membranes. That helps, of course, but it's not going to fight antigens."

"That's okay. I'm a pacifist."

He looked at me warily. "What I'm saying is this one is not very effective."

"Well it worked for me before, so I'll just take it."

I reached for the bottle, but he held it away from me.

"It also has benzalkonium as an additive, and there is some evidence to suggest it may cause birth defects."

"I've taken a vow of chastity."

"You're a priest?"

"No."

He hesitated for a moment and then said, "Oh."

He made no move to hand me the bottle, and I wondered how rude it would be if I just picked another one off the shelf. Maybe it would anger him, and he would refuse to ring up the sale. Since he was the only employee in the store, that would leave me with no option other than shoplifting, and I really had in mind starting my criminal career in a more spectacular fashion; i.e., by getting a pot from a museum.

Finally he asked, "Do you want the small bottle or the large one?"

"The large one, please."

After the drugstore, I went to a tattoo parlor. I expected a hirsute Harley jockey, but what I found was a skinny kid with moist eyes and floppy ears. I let him show me some tattoos because I felt sorry for him. He seemed pleased to practice his sales pitch. I wasn't surprised by the array of designs on offer: eagles, hearts, barbed wire fencing, Marine Corps symbols, Confederate flags and busty women. What did surprise me were his suggestions about which parts of my anatomy might be the venue for those designs. The only places off limits were my eyeballs.

I finally told him there were so many choices that I'd need to think about it. I convinced him to sell me a jar of the herbal pigments used for temporary tattoos. Their color and patina was just right for my purposes.

My final stop was a grocery store for a box of the cellophane gloves servers use in delicatessens.

When I got home I dumped the saline solution down the sink along with the benzalkonium and any other chemicals that might have been in there. I washed the bottle out with hot water and dried it by the simple expedient of leaving it in the Albuquerque air for five minutes. Then I poured the herbal pigments into the spray bottle.

Tristan arrived just as I finished putting tattoo pigment in an allergy spray bottle, and how often do you get to do that?

"Hey, Uncle Hubert. Did you call because you want a report on

Kaylee?" He went to my refrigerator and helped himself to a bottle of Cabaña. "Why do you buy beer brewed in El Salvador?"

"Because it's five dollars a case cheaper than Corona."

"I think you should worry more about taste than cost."

"That's because you're not the one paying for it. And it tastes just as good as Corona."

"You should stick to judging champagne."

"Maybe you're right," I conceded. "I don't want a report on Kaylee, but I guess I should have one."

"Well, she made a pass at me right after we got in my car, but thanks to your warning and my pure heart, I was able to fend her off."

"Not tempted at all?"

"She's attractive in a way. I don't know how to describe it."

"Earthy."

"Yeah, that's good. Earthy. But I don't think she and I have much in common. Selena and I took her to the alternative band concert last night, and it wasn't too big of a drag having her along. She actually has a pretty good sense of humor."

"How was the concert?"

"It was great. And thanks again for the loan."

"It was a gift, not a loan."

"Yeah, that's what you always say. But when I end up as the next Bill Gates, you'll change your mind. Incidentally, I think I have a new favorite group."

"What are they called, the Concrete Banana?"

"That's a good one. No, they're called SCR."

"Why do so many rock groups go by initials—REM, U2, AC/DC? Wouldn't it be better advertising to say the whole name rather than just initials?"

"Would you be more likely to buy REM if you knew what it stood for?"

"I wouldn't be buying a rock album in the first place."

"An album is what you put pictures in, Uncle Hubert. We buy CDs these days."

"I know that," I said in mock exasperation. "What does it mean anyway?"

"It means 'rapid eye movement.'"

"I know that, too. What I meant was what does SCR stand for? Slime-coated reptiles? So cool Republicans?"

"There are no cool Republicans. And it stands for 'stem cell research.'"

"I'm sorry I asked. What can you tell me about things that will detect if someone is trying to record me?"

"First a hidden camera and now a bug detector. Are you secretly a spy?"

I ignored the question and listened as Tristan started to explain how such devices work. I cut him short and ask him just to get me something I could have for a meeting with someone who might try to record me. He said he would bring one by the next morning.

31

After refreshments were on the table at Dos Hermanas that evening, Susannah said, "I talked to my boss, and he agreed to hire Kaylee as a pot scrubber. Actually, he's not doing her any favor. Other than *mojados*, you can't find people to do that work. He'll be happy to have her. The only question is whether she will do it."

"I suspect it's either that or prostitution."

"Not nice."

"Well, what other skills does she have?"

"I don't know. I only spent a few hours with her before I turned her over to Father Groaz. How's she doing with Tristan's friend?"

"Okay I guess. At least she hasn't shown up on my doorstep again. But she can't stay there long. Will pot scrubber wages pay for an apartment?"

"I doubt it. The only one of the scrubbers I know is a guy named Arturo. I think he's the only one who speaks English. He lives with his parents out in the south valley somewhere. The others come and go as a group, so I suspect it's one of those eight-in-a-room deals."

Susannah had the pictures of the pot and its measurements. She had selected a Tuesday morning thinking there was less chance of other people being around. I started to tell her you can be alone in the Valle del Rio Museum almost any time you want because they . . . But I'd done enough haranguing about museums for the week, so I let it pass.

"You didn't leave any prints did you?"

"Oh, geez, I didn't think of that."

"I'm just joking. There's no problem with your prints being in the Museum. After all, it is open to the public, and they have a photographic record that you've been there. The only problem would be if your prints are on the pot."

"Well of course they're on the pot, Hubert. I had to touch it to measure it, didn't I?"

"No problem, Suze." I smiled at her. "We'll wipe them off after we get the pot out of the Museum."

32

"Downtown Albuquerque," said Mrs. Walter Masoir, "was charming. Mind you, some of the shops had tacky names like Teepee Tailors and Dessert Sands Coffee Shop, but at least you could find a proper dress and enjoy tea in china cups."

"It sounds nice," I agreed.

"Porters. They had porters to carry your packages to your automobile." She breathed the sort of sigh that indicates longing for a lost age of refinement. "The malls ruined all that. I can't imagine why anyone would shop in those dreadful places."

"Maybe it's the parking," I suggested.

"Nonsense," she was quick to reply. "It's no good having parking if the shops sell shoddy merchandise. And all those young children running around like mice." She turned to face me. "Where are their parents?"

I shook my head.

"Exactly. What did you say your name is, young man?"

"Schuze, ma'am, Hubert Schuze."

She had come into my shop that morning wearing a tailored blue suit and a coral broach. I didn't recognize her, but I knew the name when she introduced herself.

"Well, Mr. Schuze, your shop is a delightful respite from the tawdry merchandise offered elsewhere in this city and especially in this venerable square."

The venerable square, as she described Old Town, is on a site known in 1650 as *El Bosque de Doña Luisa.* If Luisa could see her grove today, I fear she too would sigh. Mrs. Masoir was right. Many of the old adobe homes are now shops selling rubber rattlesnakes and prickly pear preserves. But several sell good pottery, although I'm the only purist who eschews contemporary works.

Mrs. Masoir struck me as the sort of woman who preferred to be called Mrs. Masoir and who used words like "venerable." When she had parked directly in front of my shop, I'd gone outside to warn her she couldn't park there. She turned her face up to me, a round face with sparkling blue eyes and a small turned-up nose, and said, "Nonsense, I can park anywhere."

Then she pulled a handicapped-parking permit out of her purse and hung it on the rearview mirror of her Chrysler, twenty feet of russet steel with a white vinyl roof, vintage Sixties. Her vintage was considerably earlier.

"The State gave me this permit because I use a cane." She shook her head as if to indicate the State was run by ninnies. "I'm certainly not disabled, but I kept the permit because handicapped spaces are the only ones that accommodate my automobile. Do you think they make parking spaces smaller these days because of all those imported cars?"

"Maybe," I said, "but you can't park here even with a handicapped permit. This is a fire lane."

"Nonsense. The nearest handicapped space is two blocks away. I'd never make it that far if there were a fire."

While I parsed that logic, she lifted her cane off the passenger seat and held out her hand. I took it and helped her out of the car, and that's how she came to be in my shop admiring my wares and questioning me. She had asked for a place to sit down, and I had retrieved a kitchen chair from my residence behind the shop. From that perch, she had been holding forth on the decline of Albuquerque in particular and Western Civilization in general.

"Are you an archaeologist, young man?"

It was a simple question. I studied archaeology but never received a degree in it. So how to answer?

Honesty is always best, so I said, "I studied archaeology at the University of New Mexico, but they kicked me out before I graduated."

Her eyes gleamed. "Did you know my husband?"

"He retired before I became a student. I knew of him."

"He didn't retire. He was forced out." She stated it matter-of-factly with no hint of anger or regret.

"So was I."

"So you said and quite forthrightly. I suspect Walter would have enjoyed having you as a student."

"The pleasure would have been mine."

She looked behind the counter. "Is that a genuine Maria?"

"It is."

"How long have you had it?"

"About fifteen years."

"My husband needs to buy me an anniversary present. Perhaps he will come to see it." She rose to her feet. "Help me with my shawl, Mr. Schuze."

33

"Guess what I did all day?"

It was several days after Susannah brought the pictures and measurements, and the pot-selling business remained as slow as continental drift.

"You worked on our project," Susannah answered.

"How did you guess?"

"That's the way you are. Once you start on a project, you're like a dog with a bone."

"An interesting metaphor, Suze. But dogs bury things. I dig them up."

Her head turned toward the door and her eyes lit up. "Hubie, I forgot to tell you. Kauffmann is here."

He strode between the tables with a championship gait—head up, arms relaxed, a smile affixed to his face. He was six feet tall but seemed taller, and he had shoulders as broad as the West Mesa.

Susannah introduced us, and he gave me a firm grip and an even firmer smile.

"Great to meet you, Hubie. My little Susannah thinks you're super."

Hubie? My little Susannah? For all his perfection, there was something grating about this instant familiarity. Then I told myself not to be so quick to judge. Susannah likes him. Be a nice guy, I told myself.

"She tells me the same about you," I replied. "Join us for a drink?"

"Sorry, mate. We've got reservations at Zia, and they hold a table for no one."

Mate? I told myself again to be nice. They said their goodbyes and left, which was just as well. Because even though I was telling myself to be nice, I don't think I was listening. I didn't like him calling me Hubie when we had just met. Then I felt guilty for being so churlish and asked myself whether I was jealous. And of course I was. I was jealous because my friend was with someone else, and I was alone at Dos Hermanas when I should have been enjoying her company.

Rather than sit there feeling sad and small, I decided to work. Susannah is right. When I start a project, I become a dog with a bone. Or a cat with a ball of string. Or a guinea pig with a wheel. Or . . .

There are many varieties of ancient Southwestern pottery, and almost everything we know about the people who made them is guesswork. Archaeologists find some pots with handles in one site and some pots without handles from the same era but at another site, and they assume they are dealing with two different groups. But for all we know, they could have been relatives who sat around the fire arguing about whether it was worthwhile to put handles on pots. Or they may have been enemies with different languages and cultures. We use the meager evidence we have to construct a theory, and then we adjust as new evidence becomes available.

The pot I was working on had a curved handle on one side that ran from the lip to the broadest part of the body. The shape was like the pitcher you see on Kool-Aid ads. Instead of the smiley face, however, my pot was decorated with the geometric patterns of the Mogollon. Some people believe these patterns were chosen simply as decoration. After reading about Pythagoras, I have come to think these designs probably had significance for the potters. Pythagoras was assigning meaning to numbers fifteen hundred years earlier, so I think it's a natural assumption that the Mogollon might have done something similar with shapes. Maybe the sides of a triangle represented earth, fire and wind. Or man, woman, and child. Who knows?

The early potters didn't have pottery wheels. They built their pots from sheets of clay. I did the same. I have a theory about their method, and I use it when making replicas, also known as fakes. I build the shape by weaving thin willow branches. I cover the shape with damp cottonwood leaves, tearing them to shape so that the irregularities of the willow frame are smoothed out. I then roll out sheets of clay and form them around the mold. The key to success is keeping the clay at the right level of moisture. Get it too wet and it slumps. Let it get too dry and the sheets won't adhere to each other. Stretch the clay too far and you get a hole you can't fix. Stretch it too little and you have thick walls that won't contour properly. It's a skill acquired through practice.

When the pot is finished, I pack it with dry leaves and set them on fire, burning away the willow mould and giving the inside the black tint typical of Mogollon pottery.

I worked hard on the pot because it had to fool someone who, although not an expert in pots, had a trained eye. The hardest part was incorporating the shard from Gran Quivira at just the right place. When the pot was completely finished, I did something I normally don't do. I broke it. Just a small chip off the rim. I etched a line around the area I wanted to break off and held my breath as I tapped it with a mallet. The piece came away exactly as planned, exposing only the edge of the embedded V-shaped shard.

I breathed a sigh of relief and examined the pot. Like Andy Warhol's soup can, it was going to prove more valuable than the original.

34

The next morning dawned clear, crisp and still. I dressed in a pair of dark gray cotton trousers, a light blue oxford cloth shirt, grey brushed-leather walking shoes and a black Windbreaker. I placed the nasal spray bottle in the right front pocket of my jacket, a set of charcoals in the left front pocket, a large handkerchief in my back right pocket and a sketchpad in my right hand. I rolled up one cellophane glove and placed it in the cuff of my trousers. Then I set off for the University.

I arrived at the Museum thirty minutes after it opened and found the usual collection of staff gathered at the front—one ticket seller, two guards, and a fourth person whose duties were unknown to me. There were no patrons present. I purchased a ticket and stepped up to the metal detector where the guard asked me to empty everything in my pockets into a plastic bowl. I did so. I thought he examined everything more closely than usual, but maybe that was just mild paranoia. He asked for the sketchpad. He examined it and placed it on the table past the detector next to the plastic bowl. I passed through without setting off the buzzer and retrieved my belongings.

The second guard followed me into the room where the target pot was located. I had prepared for this contingency. I walked around slowly examining each piece of art on the walls. I selected one that looked interesting, an acrylic of a tree which had bicycles hanging from it where fruit might have been. I think that qualifies as surrealism. I sat on the bench nearest my mark, opened my sketchpad, took out my charcoals and started a rendering of the picture. After a while, the guard approached close enough to see my work. I could feel him staring although I couldn't see his face. I imagined him frowning.

I would have been. My drawing was sophomoric. He eventually got bored and went to seek the companionship of his colleagues.

I got up and went to another bench and started another drawing. A few moments later, the guard returned, noted my changed location and left again. I guess he didn't want to see my second sketch. It was nothing but an oblong ring with some shading.

My third move took me up to the ropes around the pot. I stood there to see if the guard would return. He did not. He probably figured I was making my way around the room sketching each piece, and he didn't have any interest in watching me do so.

I stepped quickly up to the pot and ran my hand around the inside. I found what I was looking for and removed it to my left front pocket. I removed my handkerchief and tented it over the opening of the pot. I retrieved the cellophane glove from my cuff and put it on my left hand. I took the spray bottle and held it inside the pot and began to pump, moving the bottle at every angle and height I could manage. It seemed to be taking an eternity, but probably took less time to do than to describe.

I removed the spray bottle and put it back in my pocket. I left the handkerchief in place while the mist settled inside the pot. I rolled the glove off from the wrist down so that it came off inside out and stuck it in my back pocket. When I thought the mist was completely settled, I lifted the handkerchief and put it back in my other back pocket. Then, standing on my tippy-toes, I peered into the pot. The entire surface was coated.

"Sir, what are you doing?"

I turned to see the guard approaching.

I lifted my sketchpad so he could see the ring I had drawn. "I'm trying to sketch this pot from a bird's-eye view," I said, trying to keep my voice steady.

"You can't go inside the ropes."

"But how can I see what the thing looks like on top?"

"I guess you'll just have to settle for the side view. Now please step back."

I did, and he replaced the rope and glared at me. I sat down on a bench and begin to sketch the pot.

The guard hovered over me for a few minutes, and then said, "Do not approach any artwork closer than indicated by the ropes."

"Sure," I said, "no problem."

He left but came back several times. I continued to sketch until I had what might pass for a completed rendering. I put the thing I had taken out of the pot into the spray bottle. I held the sketchpad under my arm, open so that the sketch of the pot was showing.

As I approached the metal detector, I fished out the spray bottle and handed it to the guard. While he was looking at it perplexedly, I went through the detector. I held out my hand, he handed me the spray bottle, and I left.

35

The preparations were complete, the trap set. Now it just needed springing.

But would it work? There had been no doubt in my mind, no hesitation in my step as I had peeled off the inventory tag and sprayed henna inside the pot in the Museum. Anxiety, yes. Even fear. But my faith in the plan went unquestioned.

I felt the same way while fabricating the fake. It could fool anyone. I even imagined the original potter would think it was hers.

But now that the time had come to take the final step, my mind was awash in doubt. The scheme that had seemed so perfect in its simplicity struck me now as childish, a plan for a prank, not a serious heist. Make a copy, embed an old shard in it, put the real inventory tag on it, and tell the museum director he had a fake and you had the genuine Mogollon.

The plan wasn't simple. It was naïve. It would never work.

But like Columbus in the Sargasso Sea, I'd gone too far to turn back. I had to find land or fall off the edge of the world.

So I picked up the phone and called the museum director.

Brandon Doak had been a member of the art history faculty before, as rumor had it, they made him director of the Valle del Rio Museum to get him out of the classroom where he made a habit of groping coeds. He knows who I am, and he almost hung up on me before I could tell him I had one of his art works.

"Which one?"

"The Mogollon Pot."

"Assuming this is true, how did you get it out of the Museum?"

"I didn't. Someone came to my shop and offered to sell it to me. I recognized it immediately, so I bought it."

"And you expect me to believe this?"

"What choice do you have? I have the pot."

"Assuming you do, why call me? You expect a ransom?"

"No. I'm sure I could sell it for more than any ransom you could muster, and to be truthful, I gave that some thought. But I decided receiving and selling stolen merchandise wouldn't do my business any good, so I've decided to return the pot to its rightful owner."

"So now you've reformed?"

"I don't have anything to reform *from*. The pots I sell are either bought by me from their owners or dug up by me. I don't run a fencing operation. I'm ready to give you the pot."

"And you're doing this out of the goodness of your heart? You don't expect anything for it?"

"I didn't say that. I said I didn't want a ransom. But there are two things I *do* want. First, I paid the seller a thousand dollars for the pot. I'd like to be reimbursed. Second, whoever stole the pot left a fake in its place. As soon as I bought the real one, I went to the Museum expecting to see an empty pedestal, but there was the pot. Only it isn't the pot. It's a fake, and a very good one."

"You would know."

"I'll take that as a compliment. The second thing I want is the fake. I can sell it for a good price."

"I won't be a party to you selling counterfeit pottery."

"You won't be a party to it. We're making a trade. You get the real pot. I get the copy. Quite a deal for you. I'll even help you avoid future embarrassment. It's obvious this was an inside job. Someone must have paid one of your employees to switch the pots during the night. If you say anything to your employees now, the guilty one will be put on guard, and you'll never discover who did it. But I can help you trap whoever did this."

"This entire conversation is preposterous."

"Stop emoting and start thinking. I have a reputation. I could approach your employees obliquely and see who takes the bait. But that's for later. The first thing you have to do is get the real pot in there without telling your employees that you knew it was missing."

"How do I know you have the real one?"

"You come examine it tonight."

"Impossible."

"Listen to me, Doak. I've scheduled a news conference for tomorrow morning. I plan to put the stolen pot in front of the media for them to examine and photograph. I'll tell them I bought the pot knowing full well that it was stolen. I'll say I hated to buy stolen property, but I was afraid if I didn't, the seller would leave my shop and the pot would never be seen again. I imagine the story line will be something like *Expelled student becomes university benefactor*. After the story becomes public, I'm sure there will be calls for an investigation into how the Museum could allow such a valuable piece to be taken. It should be an interesting challenge for you."

"This is blackmail."

"Oh, come on, Doak. Get off your high horse and start thinking. I'm offering to return a piece of your collection and no one will ever know it was gone. Come by my shop at eight tonight and examine the pot. Otherwise, 'film at 11:00.'"

36

I had two customers late that afternoon although neither made a purchase, perhaps because I was too distracted to make a sales pitch.

Tristan showed up after the second customer departed empty-handed. I needed the camera moved temporarily so it would face my back door. I was expecting a visitor and wanted a record of his entrance.

I thanked Tristan for coming and told him I wouldn't have sought his help on such short notice except for the fact that I couldn't do it myself.

"Actually, you probably could," he said. "It's simple. You just bring the camera in here and plug it in."

"But wouldn't I have to move the laser thing too?"

"Not to get one shot. That's way too much trouble."

"But how will it know when to take the picture?"

"You'll tell it."

He extracted a small box from his pocket. It wasn't much larger than a package of dental floss. It had a normal pair of plug prongs on one side and a normal electric receptacle on the opposite side. I guess you could say it was an electric hermaphrodite. He plugged the prong side into a wall outlet with the receptacle side facing out into the room. The net result was that I lost the use of one receptacle flush with the wall and gained the use of a new one that stuck an inch into the room. I couldn't see what good this plug extender did and said so.

"It's not a plug extender. Inside the box is a little radio receiver and a printed circuit. Right now the current from the wall plug is not flowing into the new receptacle. You could stick a paper clip in there and not shock yourself."

"I'll take your word for it."

"When the receiver picks up a signal of the right frequency, it activates a resistor that opens a gate in the printed circuit and connects the new outlet to the old one."

"And the leg bone is connected to the thigh bone, but why are you telling me all this?"

He handed me an even smaller box with a button. It looked like a doorbell that had been removed from its jamb. "When you push that button, it sends a radio signal and the new outlet is activated. The camera is plugged into it, so current goes to the camera and it takes a picture."

"So it's a sort of remote control?"

"Exactly."

"Why didn't you just say so?"

He shrugged. "You asked what good plugging the new receptacle into the old one did, so I told you. Anyway, when you push the button again, it turns the outlet off."

I pushed the button and looked on the computer and, sure enough, there was a picture of my kitchen door. Then I pushed it again. There was no clicking sound, but Tristan assured me the circuit was now dead. I didn't stick a paperclip in there to find out.

Then he went over the operation of the bug detector and left, a richer man but not necessarily any wiser.

I sat at my kitchen table with a beer in my hand. I was sipping slowly. I wanted to have all my wits about me when Doak showed up. He did so exactly at eight at the back alley entrance and let himself in as I had instructed.

I pushed the button as he entered. I wanted his mug shot on my computer in case he later tried to deny he had made the exchange.

The bug detector was in my pants pocket. I heard the click of the camera and then felt a buzzing against my leg and thought for a moment the camera remote was somehow electrocuting me. I twitched and tossed the thing aside, and Doak gave me a patronizing smile as if the sight of him had frightened me.

But his expression changed when I held up a card on which I had printed, "You are wearing a recording device. Say nothing. Take the device off and place it on the table."

His lips parted and I placed a finger across mine. He remained silent. I picked up the pot and placed it on the kitchen table. The blood drained out of his face. He reached under his coat and brought out a small recorder and a mike that looked like a tie clasp. He sat it on the table. I dropped it in my glass of beer.

"How did you know?" he asked.

I held up the bug detector Tristan had given me.

"I told that idiot Sanchez this was a bad idea. Campus security fancy themselves the FBI."

"You tell anyone else?"

171

"Of course not. If I told my dean or anyone else it would get out. I only told Sanchez because I hoped to protect myself in case this was some sort of trap."

"You need to be more trusting, Doak."

"Let's get this over with," he said.

He turned the pot around slowly and examined it in great detail. Then he reached inside the pot and brought out the inventory tag, a rectangular piece of metal with a number and *Valle del Rio Museum* inscribed on it.

He sat down at the table and stared at the tag.

"What's that?" I asked innocently.

"Our inventory tag." He shook his head. "I went to the Museum after you called and looked at the pot that was there. Of course there was no inventory tag, but what really gave it away was the inside of the pot. Whoever made it tried to fake the right tone using something that looks like henna. I knew immediately it was a fake. But I kept hoping until I saw this. I can't believe this is happening. This could ruin me."

"Well, I can't believe I'm giving this back to you. And I can't even take any credit for it because we both want to make sure no one ever knows it was missing. You to protect the Museum and me to protect my ability to sell the fake."

"There's one test I need to run to make absolutely sure this is genuine."

"What's that?"

"It's a scientific dating test. I can have my staff . . ." He caught himself and looked up at me.

"You'll have to run it yourself. Tonight."

"Tonight?"

"Yes. The longer I have this thing in my possession, the more risk for both of us. If you don't know how to run the test, I can do it with you watching."

"I know how to run it."

"Then let's go."

We drove to the Museum in separate cars, mine with a box holding the pot. He disabled the alarm and monitoring system with a key and let us in. The lab is in the basement and has no windows. Once we were down there, he turned on the lights.

"I'll need a small scraping from the pot for this, and it must have some of the pigment. You can't date pure clay."

"I know that. But at least take it from the part that's already chipped so as not to further damage the pot."

"Your concern for the pot is touching," he said sarcastically.

More than you know, I thought to myself.

He scraped some material into a vial. He put the vial in the machine, secured the hatch, and we stood listening to a low hum. In about forty-five seconds, a green light came on, and a small screen flashed the numbers *900–1100*.

Without saying a word, he removed the vial, washed it out and returned it to its storage area. He turned off the lights. I followed him toward the stairs. On the left wall were shelves holding pieces not currently on display. My night vision is excellent. I selected a small Remington bronze and lifted it silently as I walked by.

We went upstairs to the dark main floor and back to the pedestal to make the exchange. I sat my box down near the wall. While he was placing my fake pot carefully on the pedestal, I placed the real one in the box. Then I placed the Remington in the box with the pot. Doak came over to me as I was closing the box.

"Do you have my thousand dollars?" I asked.

"Get out," he replied.

I did and felt guilty about carrying away a pot I had stolen.

During the planning, I had seen this caper as a challenge. I told myself museums were the enemy of the people. I rationalized what I was doing. But now that I had the pot, the reality of how I got it stared me in the conscience. I hadn't "liberated" it. I hadn't righted some wrong the Museum had committed. I hadn't honored the ancient potter. I hadn't acquired the pot by "exchange." I'd stolen the damn thing.

I didn't feel guilty about the Remington. If it should turn out that I didn't need it, I could always return it to Doak just to make him even more concerned about security.

I felt a little better by the time I went to bed, partly because I had the real Mogollon pot secured in my special hiding place and partly because I had washed down some piñon candy with several glasses of Gruet.

And on top of that, I had mastered technology.

Well, perhaps *mastered* is a bit strong. After I returned from the Museum, I put Doak's bug and my bug detector in a grocery sack for Tristan. I didn't think he had any use for either device, but I figured he could probably recycle all the little doodads inside the infernal things. While looking at the detector, I figured out all by myself that the reason it had seemed to shock me was because there was a switch that allowed the user to be alerted to the presence of a bug by either ringing or buzzing, and I had inadvertently set the switch to buzz.

But that was just the beginning of my Feats of Technology.

I checked my computer and there was a picture of Doak entering my kitchen door from the alley. Of course that had been set up by Tristan. The next part I did all by myself.

I took the plug extender doohickey and plugged it into a wall receptacle in my bedroom. Then I plugged the satellite radio into it and pushed the button with the hieroglyphic symbol for On. I pushed the Up button until I found a station that played big band jazz from the Forties and Fifties. I took the remote to bed with me and read for an hour or so with music in the background. When I was ready to go to sleep, I pushed the remote and the radio went out. A few minutes later, I did the same.

37

"We did it, Hubie!"

"We did indeed."

"A toast—to partners in crime."

We clinked our glasses in celebration.

"I have a couple of questions. First, how did you get the inventory tag off?"

"Easily. They don't want to damage the artwork, so the tags are put on with something like the glue used for Post-it notes. I knew the tag had to be inside because you can see all around the outside. The first time I went to check it out, I picked it up and sat it back down, remember? I realized the pot sat smoothly on the pedestal, so the tag couldn't be on the bottom."

"Okay, but why put the tag in the nasal spray bottle?"

"The tag is metal. It might have set off the metal detector. So I placed it in a bottle they had already seen. I figured people hand things to them like that all the time when it's something they don't want to pass through the detector, things like computer disks and cameras."

"Why would someone want to keep nose spray away from a metal detector?"

"No reason I can think of. I just figured they would take it if I handed it to them. If they had asked, I would have told them my doctor told me the medicine was sensitive to electronic fields."

"I can't believe it worked," she said. "I can't believe we actually did it. Or I should say you did it. I didn't really do anything."

"On the contrary. Your part was crucial. And I know how scared you must have been because I felt the same way when I was up there with my arm stuck down the maw of the pot."

"Especially when the guard caught you up there, right?"

I nodded. "If he'd come in a minute sooner, I would have been up the arroyo without a shovel."

She groaned.

"Tell me about Zia," I said. "I've never eaten there."

"It's in an old adobe house in Corrales with kiva fireplaces in every nook and cranny. When you walk in you smell the piñon and see the orange glow of the flames. The floors are Saltillo tile with Navajo rugs scattered everywhere, and the tables have dried chamisa in Nambé vases. It's about the most romantic place I've ever seen."

"And the food?"

"I didn't understand the food."

"I don't think you're supposed to understand it. I think you're supposed to eat it."

"You know what I mean. It's one of those places where the food is supposed to reflect a philosophy."

"Which philosophy—Platonism? Do the waiters walk around with food cut-outs so the fire can cast their shapes on the walls?"

"No, I think it was nihilism."

"Let me guess. Because the portions were so small."

"How did you know?"

"One of their ads describes the food as '*nouvelle* New Mexican.' I think '*nouvelle*' must be the French word for diet."

"More like the French word for starvation," she said. "I was dying for a Blake's Hamburger after we left. But I couldn't very well ask Kauffmann to buy me a burger and fries after he'd just spent a hundred bucks on dinner, could I? And of course we were already headed back to his hotel."

"I get the picture," I said to head off any further details.

Our drinks had evaporated in the desert air, so I signaled to Angie for another round.

"I can't believe your plan worked so well."

"Neither can I. I almost didn't go through with it. The part I worried about most was fooling Doak. The inventory tag and the successful dating test helped, but the key was his vanity. He was so anxious to remove the threat to his position that he probably wanted the date test to work so he could be done with the whole problem."

"I wish he had suffered a little longer. Am I a bad person to wish that?"

"Am I a bad person to have stolen the pot?"

"Let's not say you stole it. Let's just say you deaccessioned it."

"Deaccessioned? Surely that's not a word."

"It is, and an important one. The art history program even offers a seminar in deaccession policy. And you'll like one thing they teach. Tons of artifacts have to be given away, reburied or even discarded because of lack of space and interest."

I think I stomped my feet under the table. "See why I find

archaeologists and museums such phonies? They have more stuff than they can store or study, and they would still rather throw it away than see a treasure hunter get it."

"Feel better now?"

"I do. Thanks. Do you feel better about what we did to Doak?"

"I guess so. I do know he's terrible to women and a pompous jackass to boot."

38

Thursday morning I made a good sale. Then I lost an important sale I was counting on. To top it all off, I saw a dead man walking. Sometimes the business world is tough.

The bong announced a customer, an elderly gentleman with a trim mustache on a sunken face. He was slightly stooped, and his hands showed evidence of a mild palsy. He wore a white shirt with a spread collar and a string tie. He stood just inside the entrance and surveyed the merchandise. I recognized him instantly even though he didn't know me. He came to the counter and pointed to a pot behind me.

"I'll take that Maria."

I looked around to verify which one he gestured toward.

"It's twelve thousand dollars." I said.

To which he replied, "Will you take a check?"

Since I knew who he was, I said I'd be happy to accept his check. I watched with mixed emotions as he wrote out in a shaky hand a figure with five digits to the left of the decimal.

I bought that pot for two thousand, so I was making a good profit. But I hated to see it go. I enjoyed looking at it every day. At least it was going to a good home. Walter Masoir was buying it.

It was a rare work, late enough to show Maria's spectacular style, early enough to be squarely in the tradition of San Ildefonso. I put it in a box padded by tissue paper and felt a pang as it left the shop.

Then Carl Wilkes walked in.

"I don't know any way to tell you this except straightforwardly. I can't pay you for the pot."

I felt a bigger pang.

Masoir's check that had seemed so bountiful was now less than half of what I just lost on the cancelled sale of the Mogollon pot. And I had risked prison getting it.

"I'll take an IOU," I said.

He gave me a forlorn smile. "It wouldn't be much good without my client's money."

"Maybe you could tell me who your client is, and I could arrange to have someone persuade him to change his mind."

"Tempting. But my business depends on protecting the anonymity of my clients."

"Even when they renege?"

He thought about it for a moment. "Maybe he'll come around and do the right thing."

After Wilkes left, I endorsed Masoir's check and walked to the bank to deposit it. It wouldn't cover my tax bill, but it would whittle it down considerably.

I eased behind the counter after returning from the bank. I looked down at the laptop and realized that neither Masoir nor Wilkes would be pictured on it because the camera was still in my kitchen. I checked, and the most recent picture was of Doak coming in. I'd gone out and in the kitchen door to do things like empty the trash. But I had removed the remote and plug thing to my bedroom, so those trips had not been captured for posterity.

Before Doak's visit, I'd had two customers that afternoon while the camera was still watching the front door. I decided to take a look at them. When you have as few as I do, you cherish each one.

I double clicked the icons earlier than Doak and saw the second customer leaving, the second customer entering, the first customer leaving and the first customer coming in. I may have been distracted at the time, but I recognized both their faces in their coming-in shots. If they came back, maybe I could sell them something.

On the list of times, I noticed two that read 03:35 and 03.18. The list uses military time. It was the morning of the same day the two customers had come in.

My late-night prowler had returned. Or, worse, there were two of them. At least this time I would have a picture of the skulker. I clicked on 03:35, and of course it was the person leaving. A quiver of fear tensed my neck muscles. The streetlight barely illuminated his back, but the shape was all I needed to see. I hit the next icon just to be sure. And looked at Agent Guvelly entering my shop at 3:18 in the morning.

39

It was just past two, but I locked up anyway. There was a chill wind, so I put on a red sweatshirt with *Lobos* in silver across the front. I'm not a fan of my alma mater's sports teams, but I do like the look of red and silver. Or cherry and silver as the Lobos' PR office insists on calling it. I walked west on Central and turned north on the Paseo del Bosque trail. There's a sculpture of sandhill cranes there. I prefer the real ones easily spotted in the open fields along the trail.

I don't understand the fascination of batting a ball over a wall, putting it into a hole in the ground, tossing it through a net or kicking it between goal posts. I know sports are good exercise, but walking is just as healthy, and there are no referees and coaches telling you what to do. You're also less likely to be injured and—my favorite part—it stimulates thought.

I needed Whit Fletcher's help, but I couldn't get it unless I helped him. The best help I could offer was solving the murder in the Hyatt. After seeing Guvelly on the laptop, I didn't even know who the victim was. So far as I knew, I was still a suspect.

The spring melt had started in the mountains to the north and the river had enough flow that I could actually hear the current. My thinking wasn't getting anywhere, so I just let the sound of the river relax me as I walked along.

Then it started snowing. It was early May, which tells you how late my payment to the IRS was and also how fickle springs are in Albuquerque. Soft flakes fluttered around me and dissolved as they hit the ground. I tried to catch a few on my hand, but the warmth of my palm melted them. The smell of the salt cedars along the river and the sight of the snow put me in mind of Christmas, but just as that pleasant thought was settling into my mind, the snow stopped and the sun came out.

I own neither an umbrella nor a snow shovel and neither does anyone else in town. Of course it does rain and snow here. It just doesn't do either long enough to justify buying the equipment.

I was relaxed and my mind had cleared. I decided to retrace my movements on the night of the murder. I remembered Martin telling me how his grandfather taught him to see himself as a bird would see him, how he learned to drift out of his body up into a bird's body and look down on his human body through the bird's eyes.

I imagined myself as a bird looking down on myself as I walked east on Central the night of the murder. For me it was just a technique to focus my memory. Maybe Martin's grandfather believed it was an actual migration of his spirit into the bird's body.

I chose a hawk. If I was going to be a bird, why be a sparrow or a wren? By the time I saw myself arrive at the Hyatt, I'd become comfortable in the hawk's body and followed myself inside. I watched

myself ride the elevators and walk the halls. I concentrated on seeing every detail no matter how small. I saw the elevator buttons.
They were the size of quarters with bronze edging around a white
circle. I spotted the camera, a white rectangle on a white mounting
arm with a black cord disappearing into the wall. I saw myself going
back down to the lobby to call Wilkes. As I started to dial Wilkes'
room, I used my bird's eyes to zoom in on the number pad and saw
my finger touch the three numbers.

I stopped thinking and went home. I took the hinges off my
cabinets and walked to the police station. I did not intend to turn
myself in.

40

"You come to turn yourself in like a good citizen, Hubert?"

Well, you already know that was not the plan.

"Remember you told me you had a piece of evidence that tied me in with the murder at the Hyatt?"

"'Course I remember. I'm the one told you that."

"I think I know what the evidence is."

"You was always good at makin' up stories. Give it your best shot."

"The security camera near the elevator on the eleventh floor taped me. That's how you knew I was on that floor. I never entered the murder room, but there's no camera in the hall, so you don't know that."

"So?"

"There are cameras everywhere in the lobby. After I left the eleventh floor, I went down to the lobby to call the person I had come to see. Here's your secret piece of evidence: I think you have a tape of me dialing. You think I'm placing an anonymous call to report the murder. But in fact, I was calling the person I came to see in the first place. I can understand why you thought I was calling about the murder because I dialed 911. But I wasn't making an emergency call. I was calling *room* 911."

He didn't even blink. "Did the person in 911 answer?"

He was testing me.

"No, I realized as I was dialing that it was a pay phone, not a house phone, so I hung up."

"That's pretty good, Hubert. But maybe you just figured out we had that tape and made up the part about the room. Who was in 911?"

There was no reason not to tell him. He could get the registry if he had to. "His name is Carl Wilkes. He's a dealer in antiquities."

"Why did you want to see some guy who sells brass beds and old wash stands?"

"He buys old pots."

"Then why don't he call himself a dealer in pots instead of a dealer in antiques?"

I stopped trying to improve Whit's English years ago, so I just said, "I guess he likes old pots."

"Real old? Like a thousand years?"

I saw where he was going but said nothing.

"Sounds like you was planning on selling him that pot from Bandelier. You know the one I mean, Hubert, the one you didn't steal."

"That's right. I didn't steal it. I have many pots for sale."

"That's a fact. But if he wanted a pot from your shop, why not just go down to Old Town? Why meet in a hotel room? Of course if I was buying or selling stolen goods, I'd probably want to do it in a place no one else would be at."

"I've already told you that if I happened to get the Bandelier pot, I would give it to you to turn in for the finder's fee."

"What I figure, Hubert, is the sale to this Wilkes person fell through. Then you decided to salvage what you could and settle for the finder's fee, and that's where I come in. Normally, that wouldn't bother me much. What do I care if you steal a pot from Bandelier? I'd be glad to get half the finder's fee, let them put the pot back for the tourists to see, and nobody's got any beef. But on the same night you were trying to make this sale, someone got murdered. And you were on the floor where it happened."

He put his feet up on his desk and leaned back in his chair. "Now, I'll level with you. I don't think you did it. But I think you know more than you're telling me. It wouldn't be the first time. I can't do business with you while this murder case is open."

"I understand that, and maybe I can help. Can you at least tell me the name of the person who was killed?"

He did, along with a few details.

Then I pulled the hinges out of my pocket and asked him to have them checked for fingerprints.

"Sure, Hubert. We can do that. Got any blood samples you want analyzed? How about comparing bullets? We do that, too."

"Just the fingerprints, Whit. It might solve a murder."

41

"Guvelly's alive," I told Susannah as I sat down at our table.

"Alive?"

I nodded. "At least he was at 3:35 morning before last. He was captured on film by the security camera Tristan installed for me"

"I don't think it uses film, Hubie."

I shrugged.

"So someone else was dead in Gubelly's room."

"Right. Except it wasn't Gubelly's room. And it wasn't Guvelly's room either."

Ignoring my attempt to correct her pronunciation of the agent's name, she said, "He wrote that room number on his card."

"Yeah, which I don't understand. But I know it wasn't his room. Remember I tried to get Fletcher's help the first time by telling him about Guvelly? But he'd never heard of him at that point. Obviously, the police checked the registration for the room the body was in, so it couldn't have been Guvelly who signed in."

"He may not have been in that room, but he was in your shop, so he really does think you stole the pot."

"He must. I can't think of any other reason why he'd be snooping around my place."

"Did Fletcher tell you the name of the person we thought was Gruvelly but wasn't who was in the room we thought was Gruvelly's but wasn't?" She hesitated for a moment. "Did I say that right?"

"Except for the name, yes. Anyway, the dead guy was Hugo Berdal."

"What kind of a name is Berdal? It sounds like a generic bird call for hunters."

"So it does. Why don't you look it up on the Internet and tell me what you find." I was beginning to develop a theory. "Fletcher also told me Berdal lived in Los Alamos and worked as a security guard at Bandelier."

"I'll bet he stole the pot."

"Almost certainly. But for whom?"

"Why not for himself?"

"If he took it for himself, what was he doing in Guvelly's room?"

"Maybe he agreed to give it back. That's what Gur . . . the agent wanted you to do. He even hinted at a finder's fee. Maybe Berdal wanted the finder's fee."

"Maybe. But why kill him?"

"That's what we have to find out—why and who."

"We?"

"Yes. We're partners in crime, remember? Now that we have this new information, we need to do something. I just don't know what."

"I think I do, but I don't like it."

"Sounds exciting. What is it?"

"I need to break into Berdal's house."

She plopped her drink down on the table. "Geez, Hubie, for someone who isn't a burglar, you're becoming quite a break-in artist."

"I've never broken in to anything."

"True. You didn't break into the Valle del Rio Museum. You just tricked the director into letting you walk in after hours and switch your fake pot for the real one."

"I suppose it comes down to the same thing, doesn't it?"

"Well, I'd have a hard time seeing it as mining the riches of the earth. And I'd have to say the same about Berdal's house."

"I'm not breaking in as a burglar, Suze. I'd be going in to look for clues, not to steal anything."

"And what if you just happen to find the Bandelier pot?"

"I'm sure the police have searched the place. The pot can't be there."

"Suppose they missed it. Just hypothetically, Hubert, what would you do if you found it there?"

"I'd take it."

"I thought so."

"Well, the guy's dead. He has no need for a pot."

"He has no need for furniture either. Are you going to take that?"

"Could you use a new couch?"

She laughed. I took a sip of my margarita. I was so caught up in the conversation that I'd run out of salt on the rim but still had liquid in the glass.

"Maybe I'm just a common burglar who rationalizes his thievery."

"I know you'd never do anything you thought was really wrong. You'd never murder, rape or pillage."

"Right on the first two. Does illegally digging up old pots count as pillaging?"

"I'm not sure. You don't hear much about pillaging these days. When do we go to Los Alamos?"

42

The trip to Los Alamos had to be postponed because Layton Kent summonsed me to his table at his club. I had been demoted from a lunch appointment to a cup of coffee, maybe because my celebrity status as a murder suspect was yesterday's news.

"I know this is unpleasant for you, Hubert, and unseemly for me. I never discuss fees with clients, but I find I must make an exception in your case."

"This latte won't be added to the fee, will it?" The coffee was $4.95.

"Certainly not. You can pay for that separately."

Layton folded his napkin neatly and placed it on the table next to his cup. My napkin was nice—white cloth and larger than normal. His, on the other hand, was light yellow, made of linen and was the size of a pillowcase.

He pushed his chair back from the table and laced his fingers together on his Buddha belly. "The annual action for the *Duque de Albuquerque* Foundation draws near. Because this is the fiftieth anniversary of the organization, Mariella has decided to donate the frog pot she purchased from you several years ago."

"That's very generous of her. It's worth at least fifty thousand by now."

"I'm sure it will fetch more than that at an auction for a good cause. And my lovely bride will no doubt get more pleasure from the donation than she ever could from fifty thousand dollars."

I nodded.

"The problem, Hubert, is there will now be a considerable lacuna in her collection. If you could see your way to clear to give her a suitable pot, I can waive my fee."

"Do you have one in mind?"

"A fee or a pot?"

"A pot."

"I don't expect anything so rare or valuable as the one she is parting with. I leave it to your judgment. And hers. If she is satisfied, I am satisfied."

"Will you also waive the cost of the latte?"

He just smiled. I took that as a yes and made my exit without a stop at the cash register.

I walked back to Old Town and was honked at by several drivers angered by the effrontery of my walking on the pavement. Being a pedestrian in a Western city is challenging.

Indeed, pedestrians are rare everywhere in this country. People go to gymnasiums and indoor malls to walk for exercise, but they won't walk to the grocery store or the doctor's office. Walking is a delightful means of transportation that allows you to see what's around you. I saw a baby gopher, Indian paintbrushes about to bloom, and the tips of new tumbleweeds just starting to sprout. Also pull tabs, broken glass and scraps of fast food that looked perfectly preserved, probably because they were.

I guess as an anthropologist I should be happy about our pervasive use of preservatives. It will give future generations of diggers more things to analyze when they try to figure us out. Good luck to them.

You can think while you walk and smell the flowers along the way. Provided, of course, that you aren't overcome by exhaust fumes.

Although Martin Seepu owns an old pickup, he often walks to town when he's not on a tight schedule. His house has electricity, but he doesn't use it for much besides lighting to read by and power for his radio. The list of electric conveniences he doesn't have is lengthy—no microwave, television, blender, clothes dryer, crockpot, computer, dishwasher or vacuum cleaner.

Martin lives a fuller life than most Americans who run their SUVs around town with a cell phone stuck in their ear. Here is what he has that they lack—time to reflect, knowledge of the plants and animals with whom he shares the earth, cardiovascular wellness, a strong back, a slow pulse and fitless sleep. Martin's life is richer not *in spite of* lacking possessions but precisely *because* he lacks them.

Pythagoras said that knowledge is to be preferred over possessions because things can be taken from you, but what is in your mind is yours forever.

Of course, he didn't know about Alzheimer's, but I think you'll agree that the point remains valid.

I entered my adobe through the back door and passed the next hour placing calls to the West Coast and the Midwest.

43

Miss Flossie Martin, the Latin teacher at Albuquerque High School, taught us that Caesar said, *"Omnia Gallia in tres partes divisa est."* We joked that she had heard him say it.

He could have said the same thing about New Mexico. The plains east of the mountains are culturally and geographically akin to Texas. Most of the rest of the state has an Hispanic culture and a Western landscape.

The third part is Los Alamos.

Los Alamos sprang into existence overnight when Robert Oppenheimer chose it as the research site for the Manhattan Project. He had spent time at a nearby ranch recovering from a mild case of tuberculosis. When he discovered the ranch was for sale, he cried, "Hot dog" and bought it. Naturally, he named it *Perro Caliente*.

Oppenheimer said the two things he loved most were physics and New Mexico. He thought the views from the high mesa would inspire the scientists brought there to create the first atomic bomb.

Los Alamos is about as New Mexican as clam chowder. It's mostly Anglo and mostly well educated. Over eighty percent of the adults are college educated and a third of them have graduate degrees in science or engineering. It's the only place I know of where you can still buy pocket protectors. Their bookstore with the odd name of Otowi Station sells more science books than romances.

People in Los Alamos who don't work at the Los Alamos National Labs either serve the people who do or work at nearby Bandelier National Park. Hugo Berdal was in that second group. He had occupied a studio apartment at Mesa View Apartments, which I intended to nose around by pretending to be a prospective renter.

The manager was a friendly fellow who laughed at the end of each sentence. He took a key from a set of hooks and said he would be glad to show me the vacancy. He had skin like a camel and shiny yellow hair greased into a pompadour. He was enveloped in a haze of tobacco smoke and wheezed when he talked.

Hugo's furniture had evidently been purchased with the goal of having no two pieces in the same style. It was a thoroughly depressing place.

"The guy who had the apartment passed away, so it's still full of his stuff. Hope you're not superstitious." He gave a hearty laugh that led to a coughing spasm. Then he lit another cigarette.

I propped open the front door to get some oxygen. Despite the name of the apartment complex, there was no view of a mesa. I went to the back door and opened it. No mesa from that side either, although I did spend a little more time at that door doing something the manager didn't notice.

As a prospective tenant, I figured I had the right to check out the closet space. There were few civilian clothes and only one uniform. Behind clunky brown shoes and worn cowboy boots was a pair of green felt elfin-like slippers. Go figure.

I wanted to look in the chest of drawers, but that seemed a little pushy. On one side of the room a recliner listed slightly to starboard. On the other side was an unmade bed. Next to the bed was a side table with burn marks and a few girlie magazines.

Two expired license plates were tacked to the wall. Next to them was a picture of a young man leaning against a pickup truck and wearing an uncertain smile and a red sweatshirt with *Badgers* in fat white letters. He looked vaguely familiar.

I stared at the photo for a few minutes, but he didn't become any more familiar. He didn't look any less uncertain either. From the description Whit Fletcher had given me, I was fairly certain I was looking at Hugo Berdal about ten years ago. I wanted to ask him what he had done with the pot, but he wouldn't have told me. It didn't matter. I knew where it was.

44

"You went without me?"

"I didn't want you to miss your pay from the lunch shift. You're buying the drinks tonight."

"It's my turn?"

"It is. On top of that, I need you more for the second trip."

Susannah's eyes grew larger, quite a feat when you consider how large they are to begin with. "What do you need me to do?"

"I need you to be my lookout."

"You're going to break into Berdal's apartment again?"

"It won't be again. I keep telling you I'm not a burglar."

"Yeah, and you're not a prospective renter either. You have multiple ways of getting into places you aren't supposed to be in."

"I suppose you're right. But I don't need to break in because I can just open the back door and walk in."

"How can you do that?"

"I shoved a hunk of clay into the cavity in the rear door jamb where the bolt goes in. If my guess is right, the bolt is sticking into the hole no more than an eighth of an inch, and even a non-burglar like me should be able to pry it back."

"Why didn't you put in enough clay to stop the bolt altogether? That way you wouldn't have to pry anything."

"Because I didn't want to leave the door flapping in the wind. The manager could spot that even through his cloud of cigarette smoke."

"So why are we going back?"

"I think I figured out where the pot is."

"This is even more exciting than the museum caper because we'll actually be working together."

"Caper?"

"Don't spoil this for me, Hubie. Where's the fun of being criminals if we can't talk like those old gangsters movies?"

"Okay. Just remember if anyone comes along while I'm trying to find the pot, you have to pretend to be my moll."

"I've never even been to Los Alamos."

"That's not surprising. It's not on the way to anywhere, and there's not much reason to go there. Except there might be for you. The place has more men than women."

"I'm not in the market right now."

"You probably wouldn't like them anyway. Tristan says—let me see if I can remember this—Los Alamos is full of guys who, when the waiter says, 'I'll be your server,' think it's funny to reply, 'I'll be your client.'"

"I don't get it."

"Me either. Tristan said it's a joke. I thought you might understand it."

"Is that some kind of an insult because I'm a waitress?"

"No. It's just that Tristan said it has something to do with computers. You're younger than I am, and you grew up with computers."

"I grew up on a ranch near Willard. There wasn't a computer in the county so far as I know. What do all these geeks do?"

"They work at Los Alamos National Labs."

"Doing what?"

"They used to make atomic bombs, but I don't think they do that anymore."

"Geez, that's scary. We aren't going to glow in the dark when we get back, are we?"

"I've never heard of any problems in the town itself, but there are some off-limits sites that are dangerous. Back when they were building the first atomic bomb, no one knew exactly how much enriched uranium it would take to make a bomb, so they ran experiments to determine critical mass."

"Critical mass? That sounds like when the priest uses the homily to complain about sinners in the Church."

"It's a term from physics. If you get enough radioactive material in one spot, the atoms bombard each other with gamma rays and other little bitty thingies."

"Itty bitty thingies?"

"It's a technical term from physics. The atoms start splitting apart, and that creates more—"

"Itty bitty thingies."

"Right. And if you have enough uranium around, a chain reaction begins and that leads to an atomic explosion. So making an atomic bomb is just a matter of having two pieces of radioactive material that are below critical mass and then jamming them together. They ran experiments to gauge critical mass. They piled up uranium ingots and slowly pushed another piece close to the pile to see if it started to go critical." I eased my margarita carefully toward hers to illustrate.

"Wouldn't it explode if it went critical?"

"You would think so, but apparently they could detect the start of a chain reaction using a Geiger counter, and they would jerk back the little piece of uranium they had pushed close to the pile. Of course they had to do that before the reaction got to the point of no return. They nicknamed moving the little piece in and out 'tickling the tail of the dragon.'"

She shuddered. "They must have been fearless."

"I guess they were. Sort of like pioneers, going where no one had gone before. They were young scientists about to unlock the mysteries of the forces that hold atoms together."

"Maybe we'd have been better off to leave it a mystery."

"No doubt. But the human will to learn is inexorable. Someone was going to create atomic fission. I'm glad we got there ahead of the Nazis."

"Were they sorry they let the nuclear genie out of the bottle?"

"Some of them didn't live to see it happen. The dragon killed them."

"That's terrible. Did they know that could happen?"

"Oh, they knew. The first person to die has achieved a sort of macabre fame as the first victim of the atomic age. Ironically, his father was an x-ray technician."

"You're making this up."

I shook my head. "The son was named Harry Daghlian. He was a boy genius with an engineering degree from Purdue. I expect he knew the dangers of radiation."

"Daghlian. Could he have been Basque?"

"I don't know. It sounds Armenian to me. But he did have something in common with you."

"What's that?"

"He put himself through college by waiting tables."

45

Martin took the carafe from my coffee maker, walked outside and emptied it on the street.

He came back with a milk jug of water and filled the reservoir. I gave him a fresh filter and he added coffee and hit the Brew button. In a few minutes we were drinking coffee and he was telling me what he had found out about firstNAtions.

"It ain't no nation. And it ain't first—extortion has been around a long time."

"They run a protection racket?"

He nodded. "Indians set up to sell their wares, and these two show up to collect what they call an all tribes franchise fee. Pay the fee and you get protection from the guys collecting the fee."

"They said they wanted the Bandelier pot back. They didn't say anything about protection money."

"Far as I know, they only operate on federal land. Like at four corners, which is a good sales site. The talk is that they have some tie to an official. Maybe they're paying a bribe for the privilege of running the scam."

"So why would they scare me if they weren't trying to make me pay protection money?"

"Maybe beneath their gruff exteriors, they are true pot aficionados."

I chuckled. "Sure they are. That's why they smashed the one from Acoma."

I took a sip of the coffee. It was good and I told him so.

"It's the water. A coffee bean is a coffee bean. Don't matter if it's grown by Juan Valdez in the highlands of Columbia or Bob Marley in the lowlands of Jamaica. The only thing determines the taste is how long you roast it and the water you brew it in. The water in Albuquerque has pesticides, fertilizers and fish poop. This water has nothing but H2 and O. Coffee is just something to flavor water. Good water—good coffee."

"Tell me where the spring is. I may drive up and get a few gallons each month."

"You took our land. Now you want our water?"

"We didn't take all your land. We left you a little bit."

He snapped his fingers. "And to think we never thanked you."

"You're all a bunch of ingrates."

"Anyway, if I took an outsider to our spring, I'd probably be scalped."

"Might be an improvement over the pony tail."

He affected his Jay Silverheels voice, "Women with straw hair love pony tail."

"The pony tail has nothing to do with it. Women like you because you're exotic and have the physique of a dwarf Schwarzenegger."

"And I make good coffee."

"Yeah, there's that. How's your uncle?"

"Happy to have the two thousand."

"And I suppose he doesn't know about the five hundred for the scholarship fund?"

"No. He doesn't like kids from the pueblo going off to college."

"Afraid they won't come back?"

"Even if they do, they ain't the same person who left."

"Same for everybody, Martin. You send young people off to college, and they come back different. Some of them turn into pot thieves."

"It's different with Indians."

"You don't think a Jewish family has the same sort of fear if their son goes off to Notre Dame? Or a Basque family if their daughter goes to BYU?"

"I don't know. I just know that a lot of my people don't like the scholarship fund."

"So why do you support it?"

"Because you white guys are not going away. I'm tired of the reservation doctors and teachers being Anglos. I'm tired of having our cultural centers designed by white architects and built by white engineers. I think we can get the white man's knowledge and still save our culture."

"Russell Means say the written word is a tool Europeans use to subjugate Indians."

"Yeah, and he wrote it down, so what does that tell you? I don't give a damn about politics, Native American or otherwise. I just want a better life for my people, and I think we have to figure out how to get the white man's education and retain our identity."

"It seems to be working for Asians and Hispanics."

"They don't live on reservations."

46

"Hurry up, Hubie. I'm freezing my ass off."

"I told you to bring a heavier jacket. We're at seventy-five hundred feet. Of course it's cold."

"I didn't know we were going to be outside this long. You told me you jammed the lock."

"I did, but the bolt must have slipped further into the clay than I anticipated. I can move it a little bit with this knife, but not quite enough."

I had a thin blade against the bolt, and I could pry it almost out of the jamb. But every time I thought I had it, it slipped and sprang back. I heard it snap back for about the tenth time.

"Why don't you just pick the lock?"

"How am I supposed to do that?"

"Bernie Rhodenbarr can do it."

"He's a fictional character, Suze. Give me some real-life advice I can use."

"Okay, dammit. Pry the bolt back as far as you can manage."

I did so and she stepped back and delivered a karate kick to the door. It flew open.

"I finally got it," I said.

She gave me a withering look. "Close the door and turn on the heat."

"We better not. It might attract attention."

I took off my coat and gave it to her while I started going through the drawers.

She was shining the flashlight on the walls looking at the pictures.

"Aim it where I'm searching," I requested in a stage whisper.

She did and I got a good look at rubber bands, broken pencils, cough drops, business cards, an empty Scotch Tape dispenser, utility bills, paper clips, buttons, a broken nail clipper, loose matches and a condom.

"God, there's no wrapper on that. Is it used?"

"I don't think so. It's still rolled up."

"Gross. Why would anyone have an unwrapped condom?"

"Maybe she changed her mind and he was too cheap to throw it away."

"Oh, yuk."

"Let's try the kitchen."

We turned towards the sound of the dripping sink when I suddenly flashed back on something I had just seen.

"Wait. Shine the light back on the chest of drawers."

I'd been looking in the drawers, but what I wanted was on top of the chest, held down by the lamp. Only an edge was showing. I unfolded it, looked at it and stuffed it in my pocket.

"Let's go," I whispered, but too softly to be heard over the coughing of the manager.

He came through the front door and turned on the lights.

"You want to tell me what you're doing here?" he demanded.

"Well," I said sheepishly, "I was out with my girlfriend and we had a powerful urge to . . . well, you know, but it's too cold for the back seat of a car. Then I remembered this apartment is vacant, so I figured . . ." I let my voice trail off to make the story seem authentic and also because I had no idea what to say next.

"People usually rent a place before they start screwing in it. I should call the police."

"No," I said, "don't do that. I was going to rent it, but I didn't think you'd be open for business this late at night, so I just sort of figured . . ." Once again my voice trailed off for lack of anything to say.

"If you're going to rent it, I need a deposit now. Otherwise, I'm calling the cops."

"How much is the deposit?"

"Two hundred dollars."

I looked in my wallet and found a hundred and seventy dollars. Susannah was able to muster up twenty-three.

"Will you take one ninety-three?"

He shook his head but held out his hand. We gave him the money.

"Here's the key. I'll need a month's rent in advance before you can move in. But considering your situation, you can stay here tonight."

I turned on the heat after he left since there was no longer any reason to hide our presence. Susannah sat on the side of the bed and feigned a coquettish look.

"Looks like we've got the place all to ourselves, sailor."

47

As we drove back to Albuquerque, Susannah said, "I can't believe you touched that thing."

"Well, you propositioned me."

"It's a good thing I wasn't serious. Pulling that thing out of the drawer would have been a complete turnoff."

"Geez, it wasn't used or anything."

"All the same, I want you to wash your hands with Clorox when we get back."

"I already washed them in Berdal's apartment."

"That doesn't count. It was his thingy. You need to wash them on neutral ground."

We were following Highway 4 west. The road turns south at Valle Grande then passes through Jemez Springs where's there's a retreat for wayward priests. It continues past the soda dam and the Jemez Pueblo before meeting U.S. 550 at San Ysidro. From there it's an hour back to Albuquerque.

"Well, Hubie, you finally did it. You are now officially a burglar."

"Me? You're the one who kicked the door open. I just followed you in."

"I only kicked it in because your stuffed clay trick wasn't working."

"How was I supposed to know the spring would be strong enough to push the bolt that far into the clay?"

"Maybe you should have tested it on your own lock."

"Mine are deadbolts. They don't have springs. But you're right. It wasn't a very effective technique. Good thing I'm not a burglar. I'd be very bad at it."

"Well, it doesn't matter because we got what we came for." She hesitated for a minute and then added, "What did we come for?"

"Remember I told you about the picture of Berdal and a pickup truck?"

"Yeah, I saw."

"Well, there were also two expired plates with 'truck' on them. So I figured he must be a serious pickup guy. He had a small rented apartment and a pickup. The pot was not in the apartment, so—"

Susannah finished my thought. "It must be in the pickup. But wouldn't the police have impounded it?"

"They would have if it had been at the Hyatt, but it wasn't. I asked Whit how Berdal got there, and he said they didn't know. After they found the body, some of the investigators went to the garage and the streets around the hotel and copied down every license plate. None was registered to Berdal."

"Maybe the pot isn't in his truck. Maybe Berdal took it to the Hyatt to sell to Guvelly or exchange for the finder's fee."

"You're forgetting that I have a computerized snapshot of Guvelly entering my shop *after* Berdal went to the Hyatt, so Guvelly obviously didn't have the pot."

"Oh, right. So how did Berdal get to the Hyatt? And why didn't he take his truck?"

"I don't know how he got to the Hyatt. But I do know why he didn't drive there in his truck."

I handed her the paper I had taken from under Berdal's lamp.

She examined it for a minute. "It's a work order from Pajarito Machine Shop for a valve job on a 1997 Dodge pickup, and it has Berdal's name as the customer."

"Look at the 'date promised' entry."

"May 27th. That's Tuesday."

"Three days from now. Hugo didn't drive to the Hyatt because his truck was in the shop."

Susannah smiled. "And Tuesday we're going to claim it."

48

"What's a valve job, Hubie?"

Susannah and I were returning to Los Alamos. "I don't know. It sounds like some kind of heart operation."

"You think they'll give us the truck?"

"I don't know why not. We have the repair slip."

"But you don't look like Berdal. I saw his picture in the apartment."

"As I said, we have the repair slip. Even better, we have money. I suspect they'd give the truck to Martin Seepu if he produced the cash, and he looks even less like Berdal than I do. What I'm really hoping is that I won't have to pay anything."

"What if the pot's not in the truck?"

"Then I may be out the cost of a valve job."

"This is getting expensive for you, isn't it?"

"It is. I have at least a hundred dollars invested in the fake pot.

I have a hundred and ninety-three dollar deposit on an apartment I'll never rent. I have—"

"Twenty three of that is mine."

"As I was saying, I have a hundred and seventy in the deposit. I had a thousand, retail value, in the pot firstNAtions destroyed. I owe a legal fee to Layton that will cost me another pot. I tell you, Suze, it's really true what they say—Crime doesn't pay."

"But you also have the pot from the museum that's worth twenty-five thousand."

"Only if I have a buyer, which evidently I don't. I can't advertise it for sale with the fake sitting in the Museum. Everyone would think the one I made is real because it's in the Valle del Rio Museum and the one I have is fake because even though it's not in the Museum, it used to be but no one knows that, and I can't prove it without incriminating myself. Did I say that right?"

"I have no idea. If we get the Bandelier pot, then you'll have two pots worth what?"

"At least fifty thousand in theory. Maybe more because I will have cornered the market in Mogollon water jugs. But again, they're not worth anything unless you can sell them."

"There it is on the right."

Pajarito Machine Shop was a metal building with sloping walls and a sign depicting a brightly colored bird, maybe a scarlet tanager, clutching a tool of some sort in its wing.

The Dodge pickup was parked out front. I was glad to see a metal toolbox attached to the front of the bed, the sort with dual tops hinged at the center so that they look like gull wings when they're open. If the pot was in there, I might not have to pay the repair bill.

I showed the repair ticket to the person who greeted me, and he handed me a bill for $731.82.

"Can I start it up to see how it runs?"

"Suit yourself," he said and handed me the keys.

I started it up, and it seemed to run fine. Of course I didn't know what the valves did, so I wasn't the best person to judge whether the repair had been successful. I sat in the cab for a long while pretending to listen to the engine while occupying my fingers surreptitiously under the dash. Susannah stared at me with an impatient look.

I turned it off the engine and got out. "Sounds good," I told the attendant. "I don't have enough money, so I'll have to go to the bank."

He held out his hand for the keys. I passed them back to him, and he walked back into the shop without comment.

I told Susannah we needed to stay the day, and I took her to lunch and explained the program.

After lunch we went to an Ace Hardware and bought two dozen key blanks and a set of metal files. We drove to a city park and sat at a bench under a ponderosa. I took out several plugs of clay into which I had pressed keys while sitting in Berdal's truck.

"How do you know which one is fits the toolbox?"

"I don't. I assume it's this small one, but I'm going to make copies of them all just in case."

"I hope this works better than your last clay trick."

Keys have two features that define their shape. Slots run lengthwise down their sides. Because we had the imprints of both sides, it was simple to select blanks with the right slots. The second feature is the jagged edge. Hence the files. Well, I couldn't very well hand the clay impressions to a clerk and ask him to copy them, could I?

Using the clay impressions, I filed the metal key blanks to match the originals. The blanks were made of soft metal, so the files ground them into shape easily. I used a rough file for the initial grinding and a finer one to achieve a shape identical to the clay imprint. I held the newly minted keys up to the clay imprints and their little peaks and valleys matched perfectly.

We drove to the Pajarito Machine Shop after sunset and sat in the parking lot for perhaps ten minutes. When no one arrived to challenge our right to be there, I got out and tried the keys. The first one slid in perfectly. I turned it and the padlock sprung open.

"Clay conquers all," I whispered to Susannah.

"One out of two," she replied.

The toolbox held an assortment of wrenches, which were clearly not Native American relics. There were also two large boxes. I put them both in the Bronco, re-locked the toolbox on Berdal's pickup and drove out of the lot.

I had gone several blocks when I realized I was holding my breath. I let the air out of my lungs and started to inhale again.

"Why did you take both boxes?"

"Don't tell me I'm a burglar again, Suze. I took both boxes because the more time we spent in that parking lot, the greater the risk that someone would notice."

"And you didn't want to keep tickling the tail of the dragon."

"Nicely put."

"And since both boxes are big enough to hold the missing pot, you figured take them both and find out which one has it when we are somewhere safer."

"Exactly."

"And where would that be?"

"Albuquerque."

"Oh, come on. Now that we got away, no one can possibly know we were there. Let's look now." She sounded like a little girl at Christmas. How could I refuse?

I turned onto the next dirt trail and drove into the woods. Susannah and I each carried a box to the front of the Bronco and opened it in the glow of the headlights. Hers contained the stolen pot packed in wadded up old newspapers.

Opening mine seemed anticlimactic until a withered arm flopped out of it. It looked dead and deformed but shiny at the same time. I tried to turn the box into the headlights for a better view and caught a glimpse of a head with hair that seemed pasted to the scalp. An entire human torso was somehow crammed into that box. I thought I was going to be sick. Susannah had backed away and her labored breathing sounded like distant rolling thunder.

I grew faint and dropped the box. The entire body fell out and then straightened into its full length.

Susannah's scream would have curdled magma, not to mention blood. Mine started out just as loud and then dissolved into laughter. For what we had laid out before was not a desiccated corpse. It was a partially deflated blow-up sweetie.

"Geez, Hubie, that scared the shit out of me. What kind of a creep was Berdal? You think he was using that condom on this blow-up?"

"Maybe. She doesn't appear to be pregnant."

"Not funny. Get rid of that thing, will you."

"I think I need to dispose of it where no one will find it, and it won't come back on us as a piece of evidence."

I shoved it back in the box and threw the box in the back of the Bronco.

49

In most places, summer starts on June 21st. At Dos Hermanas Tortillería, it begins when the western catalpa blooms because that's when they move some of the tables to the veranda. That glorious event arrived in late May, and we were breathing in the sweet pea scent and celebrating our success in Los Alamos.

When Angie brought our second round, I tasted it to be certain it was as good as the first. It was not.

Susannah saw me turn up my nose. "What's wrong?"

"Taste your margarita."

"Ugh. Tastes artificial."

"Like a mix."

I got Angie's attention. "These margaritas aren't up to your usual lofty standards."

She bit her lip. "Just a minute," she said and walked away.

She returned after an animated discussion inside that we heard outside.

"Sorry about that. We used the last of our triple sec on your first drink. I didn't know it, but the bartender used simple syrup and the lime flavoring we use when we make punch for catering. Can I bring you something else? On the house."

"Give us a minute," said Susannah. She turned to me after Angie left. "We've been in a rut. It's time to add a little variety to our cocktail hour."

"I don't think of it as a rut. I think of it as a tradition."

"A tradition is something people who've been dead a hundred years did when they were alive, like eating sweet *tamales* with raisins on Christmas Eve. We've only been drinking here for a couple of years."

"Well, traditions have to start somewhere. Maybe a hundred years after we're dead, our descendants will be calling this the Hubert and Susannah cocktail hour."

She shook her head. "I like Kauffmann, but he's made no mention of marriage, and I can't even remember the last time you had a date, unless you count Kaylee. The way things are going, neither one of us is going to have any descendants."

"I may be past the age for fathering children anyway."

"Don't be silly. Lots of men older than you father children."

"Yeah, but I really don't want some teacher saying to me, 'Oh, Mr. Schuze, it's so nice to meet Timmy's grandfather.'"

"Forget that and tell me what you would drink if margaritas were outlawed?"

"Illegal margaritas?"

"This is not a riddle. Choose a different drink."

"I can't think of anything."

"How about a brandy sour?"

"What's in it?"

"Brandy, lemon juice, powdered sugar and an egg."

"An egg? Raw?"

"Yes."

"Try another one."

"How about a sidecar?"

"I've heard of that one. What's in it?"

"Also brandy, triple sec . . . oops."

"Let's move away from brandy."

"You like Scotch?"

"No."

"Me neither. Gin?"

"Not really."

"Me neither. Rum."

"I think so. I haven't tasted rum for years."

She signaled to the recondite Angie and ordered two mojitos.

"Dare I ask?"

"Just wait and see."

Our drinks arrived in highball glasses. A lime wedge fluttered in an effervescent liquid with lots of ice and a few mint leaves. I took a sip. Then I took another.

"This is pretty good," I announced.

"Change can be good."

"What's in this libation other than rum and mint?"

"Sugar, club soda and the spirit of Ernest Hemingway."

"Ah. That explains my sudden compulsion to go to Havana. But what do we eat with it? I don't think chips and salsa are a good match."

"In Cuba, they eat *chicharrones* and fried green bananas."

"Hmm. What's the backup plan?"

"Peanuts?"

"Works for me."

Angie brought us a bowl of peanuts that had red skins and a second round of mojitos. Actually, the peanuts did have red skin but they didn't have a second round of mojitos. Susannah and I had those.

While I'd been drinking, she'd been thinking.

"Hubie?"

"Yes."

"Remember you told me about explaining to Whit Fletcher that you didn't really dial 911 to report a body in room 1118?"

"Yes," I said and fluttered my eyebrows like Groucho Marx, "and I didn't call 1118 to report a body in 911 either."

"Before you told Whit about the room number, he thought you had dialed the emergency number, right?"

"Right."

"So if the police thought you had called 911, what's the first thing they would do?"

"I guess they would check with 911 to review the tapes and see what I said."

"Right. But if they checked and there was no call from the Hyatt that night, Whit would have known that you *didn't* call 911."

I realized something didn't make sense, but I didn't see what until she said, "Don't you see? Someone must have called 911 from the Hyatt. If not, Whit wouldn't have thought you did. In fact, the police wouldn't have known about the murder until the next morning when the maid went in to clean. But he told you they were down there that night checking the cars in the parking garage and on the streets. So if you didn't call the real 911, who did?"

I suppose we all have moments when we feel like imbeciles. I remember pushing a hundred-pound bed to get it closer to a ten-pound floor lamp so I could see to read. I remember wanting to leave the Bronco running for warmth while I popped into a convenience store and also wanting to lock it so no one would drive away since it was already running. I won't take that story any further.

After I remembered dialing 911 (the room, not the emergency number), I was so happy to have discovered Whit's secret clue that I let my brain slip into neutral.

"I completely overlooked that. I feel like an idiot. So who made that call?"

"It had to be someone who knew Berdal had been shot."

"Right."

"So," she concluded, "it had to be Berdal, the person who shot him or someone who saw it happen."

"Whit told me Berdal was shot through the heart. I doubt he lived long enough to make a phone call. And the murderer wouldn't report his own crime, so there had to be a witness."

50

The 911 issue cantered through my mind as I walked home. I strode past my door and down to the end of the block where I turned around and passed my door in the other direction. I made laps while I thought.

Berdal didn't make the call. Unless the murderer was using a bizarre means of confession, he or she didn't make the call. So who was the witness?

I couldn't see any way to answer that, so I tried a different question: Whose room was it?

I already knew it wasn't Guvelly's room. And it wasn't Berdal's room. But so what? I was also certain it wasn't the room of Jacques Chirac or Tony Blair. The list of people who's room it was *not* contains about six billion names and is, in terms of crime solving, utterly useless. What I wanted to know was how it might come to pass that a murder took place in a hotel room where neither the murderer nor the victim was registered.

Guvelly told me he was in room 1118. Why would he do that? A scary thought slid out of the shadows and into my brain. What if he lied about it to lure me there where the murderer was waiting to ambush me? When Berdal showed up, the murderer assumed it was me and shot him.

As soon as the thought took shape, I saw how ridiculous it was. First, Guvelly didn't know I would drop by room 1118 that night. Second, even after a margarita and two mojitos, I could see no reason for Guvelly to want me killed.

I unlocked my front door, took two steps in the dark and fell on my face. Guvelly was in my shop for the fourth time. The first two times he had come to discuss my alleged crime. The third time, I had caught him in a digital snapshot breaking in. This time I had no idea why he was there. It seemed pointless for him to search the place again.

What I did know was that he wouldn't be making a fifth visit. He was what I had tripped over. He was lying very still and holding his breath. Either that, or he was dead.

I wouldn't have been more scared if Jack Nicholson had chopped through the door with an axe and said, "Heeeeere's Johnny!"

I sprinted out the front door and around the building to the alley. I didn't have the presence of mind to go through my workshop and living quarters. I was shaking so violently I probably wouldn't have been able to insert the keys into the keyholes anyway.

I was in full panic when I reached the Bronco. I somehow got it started and raced to the University without getting a ticket or running down any pedestrians.

I parked in a handicapped space. Nothing else was available and I figured having a dead man in your shop is a substantial handicap. I started working my way down the halls of the Fine Arts Building looking in every classroom.

I was breathing hard from the fear and the exertion. It occurred to me that if any of the students in the classrooms I peered into had ever had a phone call from a "breather," they might think he had tracked them down in person.

About to pass a darkened room, I stopped. Of course the room would be dark. Susannah was in an art history lecture.

I stepped quickly inside and shut the door. The professor saw the door open, but she wouldn't have got a good look at me before I closed the door. She probably thought I was a tardy student. One with asthma.

Unfortunately, the darkness that kept me from being recognized as an intruder also kept me from seeing Susannah.

I took a seat in the back and started scanning the room. Even after my eyes adjusted to the dark, I couldn't tell one person from another. I glanced up at the slides, weird abstracts with big swatches of color apparently applied at random. I hadn't seen any of them before. Then the professor flashed a slide of a painting I knew. Or some might call it a non-painting. It was *White on White* by Kazimir Malevich, a large canvas painted completely white.

Most people think they could copy a Mondrian or a Jackson Pollock. After all, how hard is it to paint rectangles or splatter paint on a canvas? Susannah says it's harder than it looks. Maybe. But how hard can it be to paint a canvas solid white?

But I was glad he painted it. Because when it hit the screen, the big bright white space was like turning on the lights. Susannah sat a few rows up. I crept up and tapped her on the shoulder.

"Hubie! What are you doing here?"

"Meet me out in the hall."

I paced outside while Susannah gathered her books and notes.

"This better be an emergency, Hubert. Casgrail hates it when people leave her lectures."

"It *is* an emergency. Guvelly's in my shop."

"So what? He's been there before."

"Yeah, but this time is different."

She stiffened and said, "Different how?"

"He's dead."

"Jesus Christ! I *knew* you were going to say that."

"So what do we do?"

"How should I know? Shouldn't we just call the police?"

"Maybe. But I think he was murdered, and considering the situation—"

"What makes you think he was murdered?"

"I don't know. You think he just had a heart attack while searching my shop?"

"Did you check for blood or a wound or something?"

"Are you kidding me? It was all I could do to feel for a pulse, and I only did that after I heard no breathing."

"Did he have a pulse?"

"I don't think so. His arm was cold."

"Oh, shit. We have to go look."

I drove us back to Old Town. I took the flashlight from the Bronco. We crept up to Guvelly's body and shined the flashlight on him. There was a hole in the middle of his forehead.

"I think he was shot," I said.

"That's a small hole."

"Big enough," I replied.

"I mean it must have been a small-caliber weapon."

"You're the ranch girl. I'll take your word for it."

"Help me roll him over."

"Why?"

"I want to see if there's much blood on the floor."

"Oh, God," I said as much to myself as to Susannah, "I can't believe I'm doing this."

Given Guvelly's girth, he would have been hard to move alive, but as—excuse the expression—dead weight, it was all the two of us could do to turn him over. There was almost no blood on the floor.

We stood in silence for a couple of minutes. My mind was blank.

"Hubie, he's already cold and he didn't bleed on your floor. That means he wasn't shot here."

"Someone killed him and dumped him here?"

"There's no other explanation."

"But who? Why? I don't—"

"We have to call the police. They might suspect you at first, but they'll be able to tell how long he's been dead, and they'll know like I do that he wasn't killed here. So they won't suspect you once they start their investigation."

"I don't know, Suze. What if you're wrong? No offense, but you're not a forensic scientist."

"What's the alternative? You want to put him in the back of your Bronco and dump him in the river?"

"No, of course not."

"Well, do I call the police now?"

"Wait—the camera! If someone brought him here, I'll have a picture of it on my laptop."

I powered up the device and double clicked on the door icon. But then I saw that the most recent picture was of Doak. I still hadn't moved the camera out of the kitchen.

I stared at the screen feeling stupid. But as I looked at the long list of times, something dawned on me. I scrolled down all the way to the first day Tristan showed me how the software keeps a record of every time the beam is interrupted. I looked at the record from the time before the camera was installed, and I had that feeling you get when you're trying to prove a theorem in math and just can't see how to do it. Then suddenly it comes to you and all the rest of the steps fall into place. I explained it to Susannah just to make sure I wasn't crazy and she got it immediately.

We decided not to call the police *per se*. We called Whit Fletcher.

51

The story appeared in the paper the next morning. A federal agent had been shot and foul play was suspected. Hubert Schuze had been questioned, but police would not say whether he was a suspect. They called me a person of interest. Of course I've always secretly thought I was a person of interest. Because of the ongoing investigation, no further details were available.

After reading the paper, I was in no mood for breakfast. I went directly to the country club where I had been summonsed again. I had another five-dollar coffee.

Layton folded his paper and placed it on the banquet next to him.

"I can explain that story," I said.

He waved a hand. "I know all about it. At present I'm more interested in another matter. I have it on good authority that you had recent dealings with Brandon Doak."

I almost choked on my coffee. "How could you know that?"

"I don't wish to sound melodramatic, Hubert, but it is my business to know things. I represent a client whose daughter has been ill-treated by Mr. Doak. In the course of our investigations, our operatives reviewed the security camera tapes from the Valle del Rio Museum. Despite your disdain for museums, you have made two recent visits. And your lady friend also visited. Our operatives found a security guard who remembers a man of your description leaving the Museum in the company of Mr. Doak."

"I think it's Dr. Doak. He has a Ph.D."

"It will be simply Doak when I finish with him. My client is an influential individual, and with my estimable help, we could no doubt make Doak rue the day he mistreated the young lady. However, my client values his privacy and that of his daughter, so we prefer to find a private way to address the matter. Do you understand?"

I nodded.

"Excellent. Now please tell me the nature of your dealings with Mr. Doak."

I told him the entire story. When I finished, he folded his large linen napkin and placed it next to the newspaper. He sat there thinking. Actually, I think it went beyond simple thinking. I believe he was ruminating.

He finally spoke. "I assume you still have the pot that was previously in the Museum?"

"I do," I said, appreciating his delicate phrasing.

"Excellent. Have it delivered to me today. And be at the Foundation ball tomorrow night at six o'clock sharp. You do have a waistcoat, do you not?"

"I do not. And I don't normally attend—"

"Hubert," he said, looking straight into my eyes, "this is not an invitation. It is a summons. You have a theft and two murder charges dangling above you like the sword of Damocles. But after the ball, you, like Cinderella, will be happy you attended."

There is no arguing with Layton. I got up to leave and he had one last directive for me.

"Bring that charming young lady you date. You know the one I mean. She's from the Inchaustigui family."

52

"'The young lady you date?' He called me that?"

"He did. He also seems to know your family."

"How would he know my family?"

"I don't know. All I can tell you is what he told me: 'I don't wish to sound melodramatic, Hubert, but it is my business to know things.'"

"Well, I don't care if he knows Santxo the Great. I'm not going to some grand ball just because he wants me to."

"Who is Santxo the Great?"

"He was the king of the Basques about a thousand years ago. It was the last time they had any semblance of nationhood. And don't try to change the subject. That lawyer of yours is a pompous jackass."

"Agreed. But I have to go, and I don't know who else I could get as a date."

"We don't date, Hubie. We're friends."

"Then come along and be my friend."

"You'll be fine without me."

"Suze, I was in the morning paper in connection to a murder. I'll be lucky if they don't throw me out. You're the one person I can count on. Besides, I bet you look great in an evening dress."

"I do, as a matter of fact. And you're wearing tails?"

"I am."

"Well, that should be worth the price of admission."

"You'll do it?"

"Geez, Hubie. I've helped you steal a pot from UNM, kicked down the door to an apartment in Los Alamos and turned over a dead man in your shop. Going to a grand ball will be a piece of cake."

We got Angie's attention and ordered a second round of cosmopolitans, a drink made with vodka, triple sec, cranberry juice and lime juice. I had argued that since triple sec was back in stock, we should go back to margaritas, but Susannah was taking this variety business seriously.

"What do you think of the cosmopolitans?" she asked.

"They make me want a turkey sandwich."

I told her what Layton had said about Doak.

"Why didn't you tell me that at the outset? I'd go to the ball in a barrel if it helped Layton pin something on Doak."

"Umm, speaking of what you'll be wearing, you won't have on high heels, will you?"

"No, Hubert, I thought perhaps a pair of flip-flops. Of course I'll be in heels. What else would I wear with an evening gown?"

"Will they be very high?"

"Why this sudden . . . Oh. They won't be terribly high, but I don't think it will matter. You'll look ten feet tall when they find out what you've done."

53

The theme was "rodeo chic." The ballroom of the Club was festooned with saddle-shaped foil cutouts. The tablecloths were pinto pony print and the centerpieces constructed from spurs. Thankfully, the light was low.

Susannah was refulgent in a pink satin strapless evening gown and rhinestone boots. I was decked out in a gray morning coat with tails, a turquoise velvet vest and a bolo tie, the last two items suggested by Susannah.

Mariella Kent wore a gold sequined bustier top and shimmering silver see-through skirt that looked like it was woven from angel hair. Underneath it were pearlescent chaps. As hard as it may be to believe, it actually looked classy. She asked me for the first dance, and I noticed all eyes were on us. Good thing my mother made me take dancing lessons.

I assumed the eyes were meant for her, but a few minutes into the dance, an older lady cut in and whirled me across the floor.

"I must say, Mr. Schuze, you are terribly handsome in tails."

Only her lips moved. I think the rest of her face had been botoxed. She was at least fifteen years my senior, but her skin was tight, her figure taut and her makeup expertly applied. She held me rather closer than I would have liked.

She put her cheek next to mine, and I feared sweet nothings were forthcoming. "You mustn't let the press get you down. Everyone knows how classless reporters are, one step above carnival people. I can assure you that everyone here admires you. Why, I can't imagine anyone more—"

At this point another older lady cut in and said, "It's sooo exciting to be dancing with a celebrity."

I just smiled.

"I don't think you killed that awful Guvelly person," she confided, "but if you did, I'm sure you had a good reason for doing so."

I smiled again.

My next partner was a buxom, silver-haired Hispanic lady whose perfume clung to me even more tightly than she did. "My husband is a major advertiser in that paper, and I told him he has to speak to them about the way they treated you in that article. They made it sound like you were already guilty. And what if you were? Did they even mention extenuating circumstances?"

I finally realized she was waiting for an answer. "No," I said, "they didn't." And then just to keep up my end of the conversation, I added, "They didn't think about self-defense either, did they?"

She let out a slight moan of titillation and held me even closer.

And so the evening went. The good news was that almost everyone I danced with was shorter than me, perhaps because of osteoporosis. It seems that the club set love mixing with dangerous felons so long as they are properly attired.

When the orchestra took a break, I headed for the bar for some liquid courage in case the next round of dancing was like the first. I was momentarily disappointed that the champagne on offer was not Dom Pérignon. Perhaps that was expecting too much even for this crowd. But when I saw they were serving Gruet, my disappointment evaporated like mist on a desert morn. I asked the bartender for two glasses, and turned to leave with one in each hand. Plan A was to find Susannah and offer her a glass. Plan B, in case she was nowhere to be found, was to drink both glasses. Both plans were temporarily stymied by Sven Nordquist.

He wore a traditional tuxedo but had done nothing to acknowledge the theme of the event. He could at least have worn his turquoise bracelet. The tux emphasized his height, and the cummerbund his rigid torso, a fixed point about which his arms seem to flail like streamer flags on a metal pole.

His berry scent preceded him to the bar, and his bottomless blue eyes glinted with disdain. "Look at you, Hubert, the perfect picture of the bourgeoisie, a glass of champagne in each hand."

I was in a charitable mood. "Would you like one," I said, extending a glass.

"I don't drink alcohol," he said.

"Can't handle the firewater?"

"That's racially insensitive and not funny."

"Well," I said, "if you're not drinking, what are you doing at the bar?"

"I was discussing a donation with one of the patrons."

"It's a fundraiser for the Foundation, Sven. Are you going to insult their hospitality by trying to siphon off money for ARRIS?"

"The Foundation is a bastion of colonialism. I merely offer them a chance to set right some of the wrongs they have done."

One of my many faults is that I rarely give up on people. Maybe I'm a slow learner. "Sven," I said, "do you ever listen to yourself? Nobody takes that sort of rhetoric seriously anymore. Can't you try to help the Indians without making it a cosmic struggle?"

He tossed his hair and walked away. I shrugged. Why let him spoil an otherwise exciting evening? And, anyway, I was glad he hadn't accepted the proffered glass of Gruet.

Layton appeared next to me and asked, "Who is that person, Hubert?"

"Sven Nordquist," I told him, "the executive director of ARRIS."

"Sounds like a deodorant. He's been pestering our guests, and that is unsupportable. I can't imagine how he was admitted."

Then he looked at me. "Not me," I said. "He's the last person I would bring."

"I'll speak to security," he said.

I found Susannah and gave her the glass of champagne. She needed it since she was steaming.

"Geez, Hubert, I've been drug across the floor and mauled by a dozen men, none of whom was young enough to be my grandfather. Where the hell have you been?"

"Dancing with their wives."

We were silenced by the auctioneer striking his podium three times to signal the beginning of the auction. The items on offer ran the gamut from a lacquered tortoise shell the size of a Volkswagen to a chaise fashioned entirely from elk antlers and leather. A UNM sweatshirt from the Fifties brought five thousand dollars. But the big event of the evening was Mariella's donated pot. It was not the frog pot she had originally meant to donate. It was the Mogollon water jug from the Valle del Rio Museum. The President of the University was the celebrity auctioneer, and he started, as presidents always do, with a speech.

"Ladies and gentlemen. You will read in the press tomorrow that the director of our Valle del Rio Museum has resigned. We have recently discovered that one of our prize holdings, a Mogollon water jug, was actually a fake. I assure you that this discovery has nothing to do with the resignation of the director." Then he paused for effect. "I also assure you that our football team will be undefeated next year." The audience broke into excited laughter. Even though I try to pay no attention to such things, it's impossible to grow up in Albuquerque without knowing that the Lobos have a history of futility when it comes to football. So the president's irony was lost on no one.

He held his hand up for quiet. "Fortunately, the original has been recovered by Mr. Hubert Schuze, one of our graduates. Please stand up and take a bow, Hubert."

After I did that, the President invited Mariella to the podium. "I believe you all know this lovely lady." Of course there was thunderous applause. "She and her husband—I can't recall his name but I believe he practices law." He let the laughter continue, basking in it until he finally held his hand aloft. "Mariella and that lawyer husband of hers commissioned Mr. Schuze to recover this pot, and they are now generously offering it at auction. They will match whatever price is bid, and the total of the bid and their match will endow a scholarship at the University. There is one small proviso. The high bidder will not get to keep the pot. It will be returned to the University. However, you will have a plaque by the pot with your name on it. Would it be crass for me to mention that the size of the plaque will be proportionate to the size of . . . Of course it would, so I won't mention it."

More applause and even greater laughter.

The pot sold for a hundred thousand dollars.

54

"I can't believe you did that, Hubie."

"He caught me off guard. He asked me to take a bow, so I took one."

"I'm not talking about the bow. I'm talking about that Nixon-esque wave to the crowd."

"Well," I pointed out, "I'm short. If I just bowed, they wouldn't see me."

"You looked like you were running for something."

"If it was for director of the commission on aging, I'd be a shoo-in after last night."

"I also can't believe he called you a graduate. They ignored you for years, and now that Layton Kent makes you out to be some kind of a hero, the University is anxious to claim you. You'll probably get a letter from the development office soliciting a donation."

"Oh, I get those every year. Just because they kick you out doesn't mean they don't want your money. And anyway, I *am* a graduate, remember? I have a business degree."

"Yeah, but remember what your father said about that when you went back to college the second time and ended up in archaeology."

I smiled at the memory of my father. He said I got a business degree and then went back to get an education.

I had slept most of the day. I don't know what exhausted me more, the dancing or the constant attention. I was rested enough to keep my standing five o'clock appointment at Dos Hermanas, and Susannah and I were drinking pisco sours.

"These aren't bad," I said. "What are they made from?"

"Don't ask."

"Can you at least tell me what pisco is?"

"It's a distilled wine made in Chile from a special variety of grape."

"How do you know all this stuff?"

"I'm a waitress. We also take drink orders."

"Well, you may have missed your calling. Maybe you should go to bartending school."

"At least then I might have a chance to graduate."

"You'll graduate from UNM eventually, but so what. Bartenders make more than most college graduates."

I waved to Angie for a second round of piscos.

"Susannah, I want to thank you for saving me the other night. I really panicked when I tripped over Guvelly in my shop. But you were a rock."

"Thanks. You may have been panicky at first, but you certainly got your brain in gear when you figured out what happened."

"We make a great team."

"I'll drink to that," she said. "It's funny, isn't it? The pot that was auctioned off has made a round trip—from the Museum to you and back to the Museum."

"Seems like a lot of wasted effort."

"Not really. The University now has another two hundred thousand in the scholarship fund, and you got your legal bill erased."

"Yes, but I wouldn't have had a legal bill except for this whole episode. So you can't count that as a gain."

"Did you get anything else for the pot?"

"No money, but I did get Layton and Mariella's goodwill."

"Why are you smiling like that?"

"I also got my fake back."

"So both pots came full circle. What will you do with the fake? You can't sell it after all the publicity surrounding you and the Valle del Rio Museum."

"Don't be too certain about that. I've often sold fake pots to customers who thought they were genuine. This is a chance to sell a fake pot as a fake."

"I don't get it."

"Thanks to all the publicity, the UNM Mogollon water jug is enjoying its fifteen minutes of fame. People buy prints and reproductions of originals all the time. So I'm thinking of putting an ad in the paper with a picture of the reproduction I made. Even though it's a reproduction, it's still one of a kind. I think it would bring a few thousand."

"So you're moving from fakes to reproductions."

"The only difference between a fake and reproduction is in the mind of the buyer."

"And what about the other pot?"

"The one from Bandelier?"

"Yeah. What will you do with that one?"

"Fletcher's going to turn it in for the finder's fee, which is five thousand."

"So you'll get twenty-five hundred for your share of the finder's fee and maybe the same amount for the fake. That's a total of five thousand, only ten percent of what the two pots were worth when you had them both."

"Hardly worth worrying about, right?"

"I know that sly look. What are you getting at?"

"I'm not keeping the five thousand. After all, I had the sale of the Maria and that paid half of my tax bill. And I don't want to spoil the IRS by paying everything on time. So I'm using all the Mogollon-related money to start a scholarship called the Guvelly award for the top student each year from Martin's pueblo."

She smiled that big rancher-girl smile. "I think I'll buy you a drink."

55

In order to explain what happened the next evening at five, I need to describe Susannah. That's more difficult than it sounds because when I look at her I see her personality, and that influences what I see.

What I like best about Susannah Inchaustigui is her refreshing lack of guile. But that wouldn't help a sketch artist. So how do I describe her? She's a couple of inches taller than me and has that healthy rancher look, like she can ride, rope and wrestle steers. She's not fat, she's not even plump, but you wouldn't call her thin either. She has curves in all the places girls should have curves and like she herself said, she looks great in an evening dress.

But in her normal casual clothes at Dos Hermanas, she's just the girl next door, her thick brown hair held back in a ponytail, and her honey-colored eyes taking in the world like she was born yesterday.

But when I saw her the next night, her eyes were larger than normal and bright red. Her nose was glowing pink and running, and her hair was a tangle of clumps and strands. She gave me a brave smile as I approached the table and then broke into tears.

"Shit! I said I wasn't going to cry in front of you, and I couldn't even control it for five seconds."

Then she really let loose.

I scooted my chair over next to hers and she put her arms around me and cried on my shoulder. I had never seen her cry like that, but like everything else she does, she did it with gusto. After a minute or two my entire shoulder was wet.

I wanted to say something but didn't know what to say. Men are clueless in such situations, and I'm worse than most. So I just held her and let her cry. After what seemed a long time but was probably only three minutes, she lifted her head, took a paper napkin out of the dispenser and blew her nose.

"God, that was gross," she said.

"Nothing like a good cry to clear the sinuses."

"I didn't need my sinuses cleared. God, I must look awful."

I decided not to comment on that. "You want to tell me why you're crying?"

She threw her head down on the table and started again. After a moment, she muttered a few words.

"Sorry. I couldn't hear you."

She lifted her head slightly and said, "He's married."

Then she put her head back down, but she didn't cry. She just stayed there with her arms crossed on the table and her head buried in her arms. Then she looked up and said, "Shit! I don't need this. He's not worth it. No man is worth it. You're all a bunch of shits, you know that, Hubie?"

"So I've been told."

"Of course you are less of a shit than any other man I know."

"Thanks."

"Let's get drunk."

She ordered margaritas. I guess every cloud does have a silver lining.

Although she said we weren't going to talk about Kauffmann, we did anyway. Actually, she talked and I listened. The initial stream of invective was bitter and loud, but she eventually ran out of steam. Or maybe the tequila took the steam out of her. When she was well past tipsy, she looked at me and said, "Do you think I'm attractive?"

"I don't think there's a man alive who wouldn't find you attractive."

"What about the gay ones?"

"Well, you would have Marilyn for competition."

She started sobbing again. "You are full of tricky answers, Hubert."

"I didn't mean to be tricky."

"I asked you if you thought I was attractive, and you didn't answer me."

"You're my friend, Susannah. I thought you were asking about your attractiveness to men in general."

"I don't know what you're saying. Anyway, I don't remember the question. What did you ask me?"

"I didn't ask you anything. You asked me something."

"What did I ask you?"

"You asked me if you could go to sleep."

"Right," she said, "that's what I want to do, go to sleep."

I managed to half-walk and half-drag her across the plaza and down the block to my shop. I used the alley entrance to avoid locking and unlocking doors. I pushed her into the bathroom. When she staggered out, I walked her over to my bed, pulled off the covers and helped her lie down. While I was taking off her shoes, she said, "I can sleep on the floor. I can't take your bed."

"Beds are not like other possessions. They belong to whoever is sleeping in them."

She didn't hear that pearl of wisdom because she was already asleep.

56

I climbed out of my hammock the next morning with a stiff back, but it loosened up after a hot shower. Susannah didn't need my coffee on top of a hangover, so I went to Flying Star and bought two large lattes, which did major damage to a ten dollar bill.

When I got back, rain had started to drizzle. I scooted inside and transferred the coffees from the paper cups to mugs and placed them in a warm oven. Then I prepared *huevos rancheros* and waited for Susannah to wake up.

I passed the time by reading another article from the Pythagoras anthology.

Susannah awoke with a hangover. Aspirin, hot coffee, a hot shower and a hearty *desayuno* of *huevos rancheros* brought her back among the living.

I planned to steer the conversation away from Kauffmann's treachery, but the topic didn't arise. Susannah saw the book on Pythagoras and asked me, somewhat tongue-in-cheek, what I had learned while reading it.

"Pythagoras was introduced to philosophy by Thales."

"I remember Thales from my philosophy course," she said, "but only that he was the first philosopher."

"That's all there is to remember. Only one sentence of his writing remains: 'Everything is water.'"

"I guess he'd never been to New Mexico."

I was glad her sense of humor was intact. "We know a lot more about Pythagoras," I volunteered. "He traveled to Egypt in search of knowledge, but the schools there wouldn't admit him until he went through forty days of fasting and deep breathing to achieve the proper discipline. Pythagoras said to them, 'I have come for knowledge, not for discipline.'"

"Better than today's students. Most of them don't have discipline or knowledge."

"Pythagoras also traveled to India where it's believed he met Gautama the Buddha. After accumulating wisdom in all these travels, he founded a school where he taught his own philosophy of life."

"Which was?"

"Part of it was avoidance of beans."

"You're joking."

"I'm not. In fact, his death is reputed to have come when he was fleeing from rebels and came to a bean field. Because he refused to cross, he was captured and killed. But here's something about his school I really like. When a student was expelled, a tomb bearing the expelled student's name was erected in the garden. Pythagoras taught that such a student was dead and would proclaim, 'His body appears among men, but his soul is dead. Let us weep for it.'"

"I was thinking about you being expelled. Now that the president of UNM has publicly praised you and described you as one of their graduates, I wonder if you should petition to have the record of your dismissal expunged."

"I don't think so. It would be like acknowledging it was valid to begin with. On top of that, if I keep my dismissal status, the University might someday erect a tomb on campus with my name on it."

She laughed—it was good to hear—and took another sip of coffee. Then she looked pensive. I thought she was going to say something about Kauffmann, but instead she said, "Kaylee wants to get married."

"Does she have anyone in mind as a groom?"

She nodded. "Arturo, the pot scrubber I told you about."

"How did that happen? Or do I want to know?"

"After she agreed to take a job as a pot scrubber, the boss asked Arturo to show her the ropes because he's the only one back there who speaks English."

"Did showing her the ropes get her pregnant?"

"Just listen, okay?"

"Okay."

"As you suggested, I asked the boss if he had any idea where she could stay temporarily. He said Arturo's parents were just scraping by and could use a little rent. He talked to them, and they agreed to rent her a spare room. The boss is paying them twenty-five dollars a week, and Kaylee is able to get back and forth to work with Arturo. So in the course of working together, living in the same house and commuting to work together, I guess they fell in love."

I had a cynical remark in mind but kept silent since I'd already been admonished.

"It's kind of romantic," she said. "A confused runaway girl and a hard-working pot scrubber without much chance to attract a girl-friend find each other and fall in love."

Considering what had happened to Susannah, I didn't think it was a good time for her to be talking about people falling in love, but I didn't see any way to change the subject. I asked her to tell me about Arturo.

"He's a sweetheart. Works hard, always polite to everyone. He smiles a lot."

"They haven't known each other very long."

"True love isn't a matter of time."

"So when's the date?"

"They haven't set it yet. There's something they have to do first."

"Get a blood test?"

She sighed. "You don't need blood tests to get married these days, Hubert. Arturo has to ask for her hand in marriage."

"That's very traditional of him, but who's he going to ask?" I really didn't see this coming, but I should have known from the sneaky smile on Susannah's face.

"You, Hubert. Kaylee asked him to ask you."

57

It was time to make the trip I had prepared for but hoped to avoid.

I set my alarm for the second time in a month and got up in time to make the 6:50 flight to LAX. The flight was packed with business people getting a jump on the competition. Owing to the miracle of the jet engine and the change of time zone, we arrived at the exact time we had departed.

That set the surreal tone for my visit to Los Angeles.

I spent more time on the shuttle bus to the car rental company than I had on the plane. There was a long line at the on-ramp to the freeway, and once you nudged your way into the traffic, it looked like a Hollywood chase sequence. I consulted the map the young lady at the rental counter had given me—she had taken several screen tests and was there only temporarily. I avoided the freeway by taking Sepulveda north. I was in no hurry. I wanted to arrive after everyone who was going out of the house would have already done so. I found a Carl's Jr. and had a breakfast sandwich and a cup of coffee. Carl or his Jr. had a payphone. I made a call and let it ring until a machine answered. Then I hung up.

I turned east on Sunset and found the road, a steeply winding lane lined by attractively designed homes surrounded by eucalyptus, Lombardy poplars, palo verdes and some other trees I couldn't name. Unlike what I expected in Southern California, the homes were neither large nor ostentatious. They looked like they had been designed by skilled architects, people who designed houses to live in rather than to show off. That boded well for me since it meant they would likely have sturdy doors, something true break-in artists avoid but which I was counting on.

I had never done this before, but I had a plan.

I came to the address and pulled in to a driveway that curved around the side of the house, so I couldn't see if there was a garage. I parked in front and walked to the door. It was solid wood with dark stain and looked to have been custom made. The doorknob was bronze. I bent over and saw the brand name etched under the knob. I did a quick rendering of the device on a 3 x 5 card.

It was a quiet enclave with only a hint of traffic noise in the distance. Birds chirped and leaves rustled in a gentle breeze. Despite the serene setting, I was nervous. I could feel the paperboy or milkman standing behind me, and I almost couldn't resist the temptation to look over my shoulder. If I looked once, I would look again, and then I'd lose what little nerve I had mustered up for the occasion.

Because of the elevation and heavy foliage, the only building I could see was part of the Getty Museum a couple of miles away on the other side of 405. I wished I were there staring at the art instead of on a stranger's porch staring at his lock. But I stayed where I was.

I rang the doorbell and waited.

No one answered.

Maybe the bell was out of order. I knocked loudly. When no one answered, I got back in my car and drove to an Ace Hardware I'd spotted on Sepulveda. I bought fifty dollars' worth of supplies then returned to Carl's Jr. and called the same number with the same result.

I went back to the house and went through the same routine. I rang the doorbell and waited. When no one answered, I knocked loudly. When no one answered, I went back to the rental car as I had done before. But this time I didn't drive away. Instead, I brought my supplies from the hardware store and a box I brought from Albuquerque and put everything on the front porch.

As I lined up the things I would need, I was wishing I didn't have to do this in broad daylight. But I didn't have a choice. I certainly wasn't going to break in at night when someone would be home. I set to work.

I'm a treasure hunter, not a burglar, so I don't know the methods burglars use to break in to houses. I had put together my own plan, perhaps unorthodox, but it suited my needs.

I took a new lockset out of its plastic packaging, thinking as I struggled to do so that breaking into the house would be easier than breaking into the plastic packaging. I studied how the lockset worked, took out its cylinder and put the lockset down on the porch. I placed the screwdriver I'd purchased next to the lockset.

Then I took out the sledgehammer.

I checked my watch. Then I gave the lock a solid blow. The brand was Defiant, no doubt a serviceable lock, but it couldn't defy a twelve-pound sledge. It broke like a dry stick. Pieces of the lock fell around my feet with a clinking noise, and I heard other parts of it fall off inside the house.

I also heard the alarm go off, but I had anticipated that. I ran inside the house and was gone less than a minute. I came back to the door and removed the cylinder from the lock I had destroyed. I put the old cylinder in the new lockset and installed the entire unit in the door. This takes only a few seconds because all you do is insert two long bolts from the plate that goes on the inside part of the door through to the plate that goes on the outside and then tighten them up. It takes longer to describe than to do. I turned the thumbscrew, wiped everything clean with my handkerchief and pulled the door shut.

I tried it just to be sure, and it was locked as tightly as when I had arrived. I wiped off the outside parts of the lock, picked up the broken lock parts and tools and returned to the car. All of this had taken less than five minutes.

The homeowners now had a new lockset identical in appearance to the one I had smashed. Because it had the old cylinder, their keys would fit. I figured they might wonder why the alarm went off, but false alarms are not unheard of. Maybe they would put it down to a surge in the power source and forget about it. And nothing was missing, so why worry?

I had been on Sunset for about two blocks when I saw a police car with its lights flashing start up the hill. I headed back down Sepulveda. About halfway to the airport, there was a forlorn strip mall with a nail salon, a discount clothing store, a cell phone dealer, a doughnut shop and several vacant spaces. I drove around back, wiped down all my new hardware and the broken lock parts and threw everything into their Dumpster.

I had some time to kill, so I consulted the map and drove to Venice. I discovered it actually has canals like its eponymous sister in Italy.

It also had a guy playing guitar on roller skates, a panhandler advertising himself as "The World's Greatest Wino," street dancers, comedians, jugglers, weightlifters, skaters, preachers, artists, scantily clad women and even more scantily clad men.

And New Mexicans think Santa Fe is weird.

It was a depressing combination of hyperactivity and forced gaiety, the buskers pretending they like the tourists, and the tourists pretending they liked being there. I understood the phrase "alone in a crowd."

I left the boardwalk and walked to the beach. I'd never seen an ocean in person, so I decided I might as well have a look. Of course I've seen beaches in movies. I've never understood the appeal. The sand was like the sand in New Mexico—gritty. The water was too cold for swimming. The view was boring, water as far as the eye could see. I wanted to go home.

The flight from Albuquerque was my first trip in a commercial plane. A friend of my parents who was a pilot at Sandia Air Force Base once took me up in a T-28. I remember the pilot quipped as we approached the plane that his primary goal was the number of landings matching the number of takeoffs. The other thing I remember is getting airsick. Fortunately, the ride to LAX was smooth. Of course the pilot had not done the loops and barrel rolls that the Air Force pilot executed for my entertainment.

I suspected the afternoon desert wind would begin before the return flight, and it might not be so smooth. So after returning the car and catching the shuttle back to the terminal, I went to the bar to fortify myself for the flight home. In a truly upscale bar, you can specify how you want your drink prepared and be assured it will happen as you direct. Airport bars don't fit in that category, so a margarita was out. So was champagne since the only brand on offer was fermented in bulk. I won't mention the brand, but it's a common given name for French men and rhymes with ashtray, which, come to think of it, is appropriate.

I ordered a double Jim Beam on the rocks and retired to a corner table to sip and review what I had done. After being falsely accused by Susannah many times, I had finally done it. I had broken into a house. I had not broken into the Valle del Rio Museum even though I admit I gained entrance by subterfuge. I had not broken into Berdal's apartment the first time even though I admit I posed as a prospective renter. And I hadn't broken in the second time either—although I was trying to— because Susannah herself had kicked the door open. But no one had been with me today. I had not tricked anyone. I had plainly and simply, without any delusion or assistance, broken into a house. I was now a burglar.

But wait! I wasn't really a burglar because I hadn't stolen anything. That made me feel better. That and the second double bourbon.

I thought about the cactus scent and botanic overtones of tequila and how it resonates with the desert. I didn't know what resonates with California. Wine, I guess, but I don't like wine except when it has bubbles.

Bourbon was right for the moment. The woodsy smell and smoky flavor comforted me like a familiar jacket on a cold night. So I had a third. Or was it a sixth? They were doubles after all.

Whatever the number was, I could have purchased an entire

bottle in New Mexico for less. But I wasn't in New Mexico. I was about to get on a plane where the seats are uncomfortable even if you're only five six, and I needed fortification.

As we bounced and lurched through the sky, I made a mental note never to fly again.

58

I got back before five but was in no shape to meet Susannah for drinks, so I called and left a message. I topped a fried corn tortilla with refried beans, diced tomatoes, sliced jalapeños and fresh cilantro. Sort of a giant nacho. Despite the bourbon and the bumpy flight, I risked a cold beer. It seemed to have a medicinal effect.

The weather had turned warmer, so I climbed into my hammock to rest. I fell asleep and awoke around midnight to the smell of damp chamisa and the feel of light cool rain on my face. I stumbled inside and slept for another eight hours. After my usual shower and my usual breakfast, I was ready for my meeting with Kaylee and Arturo.

I asked Arturo to wait in the shop and tell me if any customers came in. I took Kaylee back to my living quarters.

"Is there anything you want to tell me about your former life in Texas?"

"No."

"You're not a fugitive from justice? The police aren't looking for you?"

"No."

"How about someone who's not a policeman? A former boyfriend, a parent, a social worker or parole officer."

"Hubert, I'm not a criminal."

"Okay, what are you?"

She looked into my eyes. "I'm just a high school dropout from Texas who was in a bad situation. One day it got worse, and I ran away. I didn't plan it. I just walked out the door and started hitching west. I've never planned anything in my life. I didn't plan to drop out of school. I just got tired of failing, so I quit going. I didn't plan to work as a waitress. I just saw a sign and went in. I didn't plan to get involved with who I got involved with. He just walked in the diner one day and I left with him after work."

She lowered her head and started crying.

"I'm sorry to make you dredge up sad memories."

She looked up at me and she was smiling. "I'm not sad, Hubert. I'm happy. These are tears of joy. For the first time in my life, I have a plan. I want to marry Arturo, work my way up to waitress, and make enough money so that we can get a place of our own. Maybe someday I'll be so rich I can buy one of your pots."

"Do you love Arturo?"

"I don't know what love is. He's a very nice person, and I like to be with him. Isn't that enough?"

"I guess so. Can you go out and ask Arturo to come in and watch the place while he's here."

"Remember the first time I came here? I offered to watch the shop, but you didn't trust me."

I didn't know what to say, so I said nothing. She got up, and I stood up out of habit. She thrust herself against me and gave me a wet kiss. Then she stepped back with a big smile and said, "Just wanted you to get a hint of what you passed up." I think it was that sense of humor Tristan mentioned.

Arturo was shorter than me, about Kaylee's height, and slight of build. He had smooth light brown skin, big damp eyes and a long horsey face. Underneath the big smile was a look of apprehension. He shook my hand limply. I sat down, but he remained standing.

"Mr. Schuze," he began, and I smiled because he pronounced it "choose," which struck me as charmingly unsophisticated. "I am here today," he continued quite formally, "to ask for the hand of Kaylee."

I realized he had been holding his breath, and now that he got out the line he memorized, he let out a long sigh.

"Do you love her?"

"More than anything in the world. She is the most beautiful girl I ever see, and she is the first girl who is ever nice to me."

I stood up and offered my hand again. "Congratulations," I said.

He ran out to the front and they were gone.

59

Old town has twenty-four businesses classified as galleries, nine gift or souvenir shops, fourteen jewelers, an equal number of "specialty shops" and thirteen eating establishments from coffee joints to upscale restaurants.

What binds us together is architecture, low adobe buildings with odd angles and organic shapes, hidden patios, brick paths, small gardens, wooden balconies and wrought-iron benches. And over three hundred years of history.

The center of it all is the gazebo, half bandstand, half Danish wedding cake, a quirky construction on an adobe base with a hexagonal roof. Or maybe it's octagonal. The wooden posts seem misaligned with the roof they support, so not even Pythagoras could figure the angles.

The finials are Victorian gingerbread and the eclectic theme is topped off by a cupola that would be right at home on top of a lighthouse.

Something is usually happening under the gazebo, be it a band concert or a political debate.

On this day, it was a wedding.

Arturo and Kaylee stood in front of a justice of the peace who made short work of pronouncing them man and wife.

Father Groaz was there along with Whit Fletcher, Tristan and his neighbor Emily. But the largest contingent was the staff from La Placita. The pot scrubbers and busboys were dressed in clean white *guayaberas*, and they had taken up a collection to pay for a mariachi band called *Los Lobos Solitarios* who led a procession to the restaurant playing *Las Mañanitas*.

I listened to the slow melodic thumping of the *guitarrón*, heard the plaintive voices of the singers and the staff who joined in, and smelled the scent of roasting chilies and frying tortillas wafting from the kitchen. I silently thanked the fates for letting me be born in Albuquerque.

The wedding buffet started with a series of toasts each followed by a shot of tequila. The toasts were almost all in Spanish, so I had to translate for Susannah, which was a good thing because otherwise I might have been throwing back tequila shots.

The buffet spread was simple: *guacamole, flautas, salsa, chalupas, carnitas, chile con queso*, and a mountain of chips, both blue corn and yellow. And of course there were *biscochitos* for dessert. There also, sitting incongruously amid the traditional dishes, was a steaming chafing dish full of Summer Squash Pie courtesy of *Nuestra Señora de Los Casseroles*. Miss Gladys Claiborne explained to me, although I had not asked, that the ingredients were frozen sliced yellow squash, sautéed yellow onions, Kraft parmesan cheese from the green cylindrical cardboard container, pulverized Ritz crackers, three strips of bacon crumbled up, and the fat left over from frying the bacon. Much to my amazement, the kitchen crew all had seconds. It must have been the bacon grease.

Miss Gladys Claiborne held up the dish for me to examine. "Would you just look at this? Those Mexican boys picked this dish so clean I won't even have to wash it!" She was a contented woman.

When finally the happy couple was set to depart on their overnight honeymoon, the pot scrubbers and busboys paraded by the couple, each accepting a peck on the cheek from Kaylee and stuffing as many ones and fives into Arturo's coat pocket as they could afford.

"Don't you want to kiss the bride?" asked Susannah.

"I already have," I replied.

As the party broke up, Fletcher and I discussed the logistics of a meeting for the next night in my shop. I gave him the list of people we needed there. He returned my hinges and told me there were no fingerprints on them.

I walked home and reinstalled the hinges on my cabinets. Then I read the last article in the Pythagoras anthology. The other ones had been about Pythagoras' life and philosophy. The last one was about his mathematics. I wasn't sure if I would be able to follow it. It had been a long time since I studied math.

You may recall from your high school math that the Pythagorean Theorem says that the square of the long side of a right triangle is equal to the sum of the squares of the two shorter sides. It doesn't really matter if you remember that. The important thing about Pythagoras' discovery is not the formula itself—it's the fact that there *is* a formula.

Pythagoras was the first human to see that there are universal patterns. Those unfailing regularities allow us to do everything from calculating the interest on a savings account to sending rockets to the moon.

We may wear different clothes, worship different deities, speak different tongues and eat different foods, but we are all held on Earth by the force of gravity, which is the same from Albuquerque to Albania.

Pythagoras was the first person to discover the regularities behind the immense variety of everyday experience. As I followed the logic of his proof of the theorem that eventually came to bear his name, I became so absorbed in the reasoning that I forgot all about murders and police.

I am awe-inspired by Pythagoras' insight. You may find it confusing or even boring. Some people are awe-inspired by majestic mountains, some by poetry and others by abstruse mathematics. But whatever the source, we all need a little awe in our lives.

60

"You all set for the big night tomorrow, Hubie?"

"I am."

"Nervous?"

"A little. But I took my mind off it by reading another article about Pythagoras."

"Geez, how much of that can you stand? You seem like a normal person in most other respects."

"Thanks, I think. Actually, I'm all through with Pythagoras for now."

"So what will you read next?"

"There's a book called *Longitude* I've been wanting to read."

"What's it about?"

"It's about how an English clockmaker solved the problem of how sailors in the middle of the ocean can figure out what longitude they're on."

"Wow, that sounds really exciting, Hubert," she said sarcastically. "And why would you care? You never travel anyway."

"I travel everywhere, Susannah. *There is no frigate like a book.*"

"That's a poem, right?"

I recited it for her:

There is no Frigate like a Book
To take us Lands away,
Nor any Coursers like a Page
Of prancing Poetry—
This Traverse may the poorest take
Without oppress of Toll—
How frugal is the Chariot
That bears a Human Soul—

"It doesn't scan very well, does it?" she observed.

"Maybe it was the way I read it."

"Maybe. But it still seems strange to worry about longitude when you'll never be on a real frigate."

"Or a courser, whatever that is. But look at it this way. I couldn't go to the stars even if I did travel, but I still care about where they are."

"Come on, Hubie, read something normal for a change. I can lend you one of my burglar books."

"I keep telling you, Suze, I'm not a burglar."

She laughed. "They're not how-to books. They're fun murder mysteries where the crime is solved by a burglar."

"I know that. You've told me about them before. I've just never read one."

"Why don't you try one? I have them all."

"Which one do you recommend?"

"How about *The Burglar in the Closet*?"

"Is that some sort of suggestion about my sexuality?"

"Huh? Oh, I get it. Well, how about *The Burglar Who Read Spinoza*? You told me you read Spinoza."

"Does it really involve Spinoza?"

"Well, it's a murder mystery, not a philosophy book, but Spinoza does play a part in it. It's a great read."

"Okay, I'll try it."

"Good. Because if you read only that serious stuff, you'll become dull, and drinking with you won't be any fun."

"I promise to read it."

"Maybe if you read more mysteries, you would have figured out these pot murders earlier."

"I doubt it. I read Pythagoras and still couldn't figure out what the murderer's angle was."

"Huh?"

"Never mind."

"Well, you did figure out the murders. That's the important thing. Oh, I almost forgot. I looked up the name Berdal on the Internet like you asked me to. I found out what sort of name it is, but I had guessed that before I looked it up."

"How?"

"Because the sweatshirt he had on in that picture of him we saw in his apartment."

"I remember that sweatshirt. It said "Badgers." Are you telling me Berdal is the name of a mammal?"

"No, silly, the Badgers are a football team. They wear the colors that the shirt had—red and white." Then she told me what sort of name Berdal is.

"How do you know stuff like football mascots?"

"Hubie," she said, "doesn't it strike you as interesting that you know nothing about football and I know nothing about cooking?"

"So much for gender stereotyping."

"Then you won't mind if I buy you a drink." She waved for Angie.

61

The crowd in my shop the next evening included Susannah, Carl Wilkes, Tristan, Layton Kent and one of his paralegals, all of whom had volunteered to be there. They were seated in a row of chairs facing my counter.

A second row included the two thugs from firstNAtions, whose names, I had since discovered, were Masho Crow, the big guy, and Dillon Smith, the bowling ball. Sven Nordquist was also present, sitting off to one side, his cerulean eyes staring ahead but aimed at nothing. Crow, Smith, and Nordquist were not volunteers but had been persuaded to come by Whit Fletcher, an imposing figure who can be pretty persuasive when he wants to be.

Of course having a gun and a badge helps.

Whit Fletcher and three uniformed policemen stood behind the chairs near the front door.

Finally, there was Reggie West, whom I had asked to bring some of his ice cream parlor chairs so we would have enough seating.

Cold dry air had spilled down from the Sandias to replace what the sun had heated earlier in the day, but I felt uncomfortably warm.

It was nerves. I hoped to unmask a couple of murderers.

To help me relax, I started with that hackneyed phrase, "You're probably wondering why I called you all together."

Tristan and Susannah laughed. The others just stared at me. Instead of being more relaxed, I was more nervous.

I began to lay it out. "A few weeks ago, a man walked into my shop and asked if there was any way for him to acquire the Mogollon pot on display at the Valle del Rio Museum. His name is Carl Wilkes, and he is the gentleman with the beard seated to my left. Mr. Wilkes' inquiry may strike you as strange, but in my line of business, it isn't unusual. Evidently, someone helped him acquire the pot because it was subsequently taken from the Museum. As you may have read in the press, the pot has now been returned thanks to Mr. Layton Kent who is seated next to Mr. Wilkes."

I paused to take a breath and to compliment myself for not "going up on my lines" as they say in the theater.

"Mr. Wilkes' visit became more intriguing when a second man came to my shop the very next day, a federal agent named Guvelly. He was investigating the theft of a pot just like the one Wilkes had asked about. The second pot had been stolen from the headquarters building in Bandelier National Park. The fact that Guvelly inquired about the Bandelier pot the day after Wilkes asked about a similar pot at the University started me thinking. Those two pots are the only known Mogollon water jugs. It could not be coincidence that one was stolen and someone wanted to acquire the other."

I had set the scene. That was easy because I was just relating facts. Now I had to explain what I thought about the facts. I wanted to lead them along my path of reasoning so they would agree with me when I sprung the names of the murderers.

"I had to start from the premise that one person wanted both pots. I could think of only three options. The first possibility is a wealthy collector who wants the pots badly enough to pay a high price and break the law even though he will never be able to display them publicly or be acknowledged as their owner. Because I sell ancient pots, I've dealt with many reclusive collectors. They have a high aversion to risk. And who can blame them? If you had a display room in your house full of ill-gotten pots, you would be careful who knew about it. If you wanted to add the two Mogollon pots to your collection, the one thing you would *not* do is hire a different person to get each pot. That doubles the risk. I ascertained that Mr. Wilkes had no participation in the theft at Bandelier, so that ruled out a collector since no collector would approach getting the two pots in that way.

"That brings us to the second possibility: someone stealing the pots for money. But an ancient pot is not like jewelry, which can easily be fenced. The only market for these pots would be the collectors we just ruled out. If those collectors are cautious about who they hire to acquire specimens for them, imagine how much more cautious they would be if a stranger shows up wanting to sell them a pot. There is no telling what sort of trail the stranger may have left. It is extremely unlikely that a collector would deal with an unknown thief."

"What would motivate a theft other than money?" asked Fletcher.

"More money," answered Susannah as if I had asked a riddle.

I ignored her and gave a one-word answer: "Politics."

Susannah looked at me with a "Here you go again" expression. Fletcher furrowed his brow. Layton turned to Sven Nordquist who continued to stare at something no one else could see. Masho Crow and Dillon Smith glanced at each other and smiled.

Reggie West said, "Politics?"

"Yes, politics. Specifically, the politics of groups struggling to overcome the marginalization of Native Americans. Most of you probably remember the American Indian Movement, also known as AIM. Their method was to call attention to the plight of Native Americans by outrageous actions designed to maximize press coverage. They painted Plymouth Rock red, seized Alcatraz Island and held a sit-in at Wounded Knee."

"You going to blame the Bandelier theft and the murders on AIM?" asked Fletcher sarcastically.

"No. But representatives from two other Native American organizations are here tonight. One is called firstNAtions, and its representatives are Masho Crow and Dillon Smith, the two gentlemen seated to my right. They came to this shop demanding that I relinquish the Bandelier pot. Had they been involved in the theft at Bandelier, they would have known that I didn't have the pot, so I ruled them out. The second group is called ARRIS, represented by Sven Nordquist, the person in the dark suit sitting off to the side of the second row."

He was staring at one of my *vigas.*

"What had been merely a theft became a more serious crime when a person by the name of Hugo Berdal was murdered in a guest room at the Hyatt. I had gone to the Hyatt to see Mr. Wilkes and just happened to be there at the time of the murder. The police at first thought I might be involved, but thanks to their investigative skill, they were able to determine my innocence."

"Cut the bull, Hubert, and get on with the story," said Fletcher.

"Mr. Berdal was a security guard at Bandelier. The missing pot was later found in Mr. Berdal's vehicle, so we can safely assume that he stole the pot. I think we can also safely assume that his murder was related to the theft."

Everyone seemed to be paying closer attention. My nerves had calmed down. Now that they were engaged in the story, I was almost enjoying leading them to its conclusion.

"The question is, why did Berdal steal the pot? I have seen his apartment and know something about his lifestyle. He was not a connoisseur of pottery. One should not speak ill of the dead, but Hugo Berdal was an uneducated loner in a minimum wage job. He probably lacked the imagination to conceive the crime, and even had he done so, he would not have known how to fence the pot. Indeed, he would have been unaware of its value. We can therefore assume he was hired to steal the pot. The question is who paid him to steal it, and the answer is that you did, Sven."

His eyes left the *viga* and focused on me. "That's ridiculous." His eyes turned a deeper shade of indigo, almost blue-black.

I couldn't hold his gaze, so I looked at the others. "It must have seemed like a simple plan. A security guard has unfettered access to the pot. He steals it for a fee and passes it to Sven who uses it for political purposes. Given the bizarre politics of ARRIS, it's difficult to guess what that purpose might be. They could hold a press conference saying they had liberated a Native American artifact from the white man's museum. When the Park Service sues to have the pot returned, ARRIS is suddenly center-stage in a drama the media would love."

"You don't know what you're talking about," said Sven, oblivious to the rest of the room, his eyes still fixed on me.

"Maybe not," I admitted, "but whatever you wanted the pot for, getting your hands on it proved to be more difficult than you anticipated when Berdal realized he was being played for a sucker. The police found a cash deposit to his checking account for five hundred dollars just days before the pot was stolen, so it's a pretty good guess that's what you paid him. Of course Guvelly questioned Berdal. It would be routine for the investigating agent to question the security staff. My guess is that during that questioning session, Guvelly mentioned how valuable the pot was. When Berdal learned the true value of the pot, he realized the five hundred was chump change. So he came to you, Sven, demanding more money. You refused. And why not? Berdal had no bargaining power at that point. What could he do? Return the pot? But then I'm guessing Hugo told you he would take the pot to Guvelly to get the finder's fee. Guvelly tried to lure me with that fee, so I suspect he mentioned it to everyone in hopes that the thief would return the pot or that someone who knew the thief would take the pot from him and return it."

Sven folded his arms over his chest. "This is all conjecture."

"I agree. But this is not conjecture. Carl Wilkes told me you asked him to get the pot from the Museum. That establishes your interest in at least one of the pots. But you didn't ask him to get the Bandelier pot because you already had someone who could do that. Hugo Berdal was your cousin."

There were gasps and squeaking chairs as everyone turned to look at Sven. He unfolded his lean arms and held them slightly aloft, taking in the crowd with a casual glance.

"So what? Being related to that philistine is unfortunate, but not a crime."

"But paying someone to steal *is*," I said. "And so is murder. When

Berdal told you he was going to see Guvelly, you probably tried to talk him out of it. Maybe you offered him more money. But he was already suspicious of you because you didn't pay him enough. So you decided to protect your investment by going with him. I'll wager you told Berdal you would top whatever Guvelly offered. Were you surprised when Hugo agreed to let you go along?"

Sven glared at me.

"Maybe you didn't know it, but his truck was in the shop, so he needed a ride anyway. That's probably why he took you up on your offer. So you took him to the Hyatt. The room Berdal and Guvelly had agreed to meet in was registered in the name of Masho Crow, whom you all met a few minutes ago. Guvelly knew he could use the room because he and Mr. Crow were conducting other business that we need not go into here."

I didn't want to divert attention from the train of reasoning by bringing up the protection racket that Guvelly was being paid not to see. And anyway, Crow had been granted immunity for his future testimony against Nordquist, so there was no reason to make his criminal activities public.

I could see the finish line. "You and Hugo arrived early for the meeting. Mr. Crow let you into the room, told you Guvelly would be along soon and left."

"He's lying," Sven squealed, his icy self-control crumbling.

Crow turned deadpan to Nordquist, and Sven sunk further into his seat.

"I don't know what happened in that room," I continued, "but my guess is you and Hugo got into an argument while waiting for Guvelly. Maybe Hugo drew his gun because he was afraid of you. Maybe you took it from him. Maybe there was a struggle. We'll never know what happened in that room unless you tell us. But what we do know is Berdal ended up dead and you called 911 and reported the murder."

He seemed to regain his confidence. "Why would I do that if I murdered him?"

"Because you were hoping to throw suspicion on Guvelly. You didn't know it wasn't his room. It seemed like a stroke of genius because if Guvelly was being investigated for murder, he wouldn't have much time or interest in searching for the missing pot. You would be home free. But even though calling 911 seemed like a good idea at the time, it turned out to be a big mistake. They have your call on tape. I'm sure your voice print will match."

"This is nonsense," said Sven. He looked around the room at the others, particularly at Fletcher. "He's trying to frame me because I'm the one who reported his theft of protected artifacts from an excavation site. It's a matter of public record. He's a thief. He was expelled from UNM because of it. You can't believe anything he says. He steals the heritage of America's indigenous peoples. He's a prototypical European, rapacious and genocidal. He's . . . he's . . ."

"Not listening," I said. "And neither is anyone else."

Sven started to rise from his chair.

"Sit down," ordered Fletcher.

As Sven slumped back into his chair, I looked up to see Miss Gladys Claiborne staring at the tableau through the window. She held up a tray and waved.

I walked to the door and pointed down to the Closed sign. She held the tray up higher and it wobbled slightly. Fearing that she was about to drop the tray, I opened the door and said, "I'm sorry Miss Gla—"

"Heavens to Betsy," she said walking past me. "Let me put this thing on the counter." And she did. Then she removed the cloth and revealed a circle of cut-crystal bowls full of dips around a mound of crackers and chips in the middle.

"I saw you were having people over, so I decided to bring some treats," she said. "This one is spicy Cajun shrimp dip. My late husband just adored it. This one is artichoke and Parmesan. This one is a true original made from onion soup mix, chow-chow and sour cream. It hasn't got a name, but don't let that stop you. It's heavenly. And let's see, what's this last one? Oh yes, this is the pecan and peaches dip. Did you ever hear of anything like that? I swear it's better than it sounds." Then she looked around the room. "Mr. Schuze, do you want to introduce your guests?"

Before I could do that, Whit Fletcher said, "Ma'am, I'm going to have to ask you to leave. We're in the middle of a police matter here, and—"

"Oh, heavens, I can see that. Why just look at those three handsome young policemen. I know they could use some nourishment."

Whit looked at me and I shrugged. Then he turned to Sven and said, "Sven Nordquist, you are under arrest for the murder of Hugo Berdal. You have the right to remain silent. You . . ."

It was the first time I had ever seen Miss Gladys Claiborne at a loss for words. All she could manage was, "Oh, my."

62

When Fletcher finished reading Sven his rights, everyone except Sven and the cop who had cuffed him began sampling the dips, and it looked as if the meeting might turn into a social event.

But Layton Kent said, "What about the second murder, Detective Fletcher. Are you going to charge Mr. Nordquist with that as well?"

Whit scooped a large dollop of spicy Cajun shrimp dip onto a cracker and said, "Everybody take your seats, and let's finish hearin' what our friend Hubert has to say."

People grabbed one more bite and returned to their seats.

"Mr. Wilkes," I said, "after Mr. Nordquist commissioned you to get the pot from the Valle del Rio Museum, did you do anything illegal in pursuit of that commission?"

"I did not."

I remembered when I asked Wilkes at the Hyatt whether Martin told him I dug up pots, he said, "No, someone else told me." I now realized that someone else was Sven Nordquist.

"What happened after you accepted his offer?"

"The pot from the Museum became available. I reported this to Mr. Nordquist, but he told me his organization had suffered some financial reversals. I reported this back to the person who had the pot at the time. As everyone knows by now, the pot was returned to the Museum."

"You may be wondering," I said, "why ARRIS would want both pots. Sven, do you want to enlighten us on that?"

I took his clinched jaw as a no.

"My guess is they thought that having the only two known intact Mogollon water jugs would be just the kind of stunt to put them on the map and bring in support and money. It was their last-gasp effort at survival. There remains now only the matter of the murder of Agent Guvelly."

"That should be easy," said Reggie. "Nordquist must have murdered Guvelly. A dead Agent Guvelly can't defend himself against the charge of murdering Berdal, so Nordquist is off the hook. And no one will suspect him of murdering Guvelly because the two of them have no connection." He smiled that winning smile of his. "Can I take my chairs and go home now?"

"That's a good theory, Reggie, but it didn't work that way. And you of all people know that because *you* murdered Guvelly."

"Come on, Hubie. Don't even joke about something like that."

"I'm not joking."

"That's crazy, man. I mean, I'm only here because you wanted to borrow a few chairs. I have nothing to do with any of these people, and you accuse me of murder? Why would you do that?"

"Because you did it. After Guvelly accused me of stealing the pot from Bandelier, he went around trying to get evidence from people here in Old Town who know me. I know this because Angie from Dos Hermanas told me about it. So did Miss Claiborne. Guvelly must have talked to you, too, Reggie. But unlike Angie and Gladys, you didn't say anything to me. That's because you saw it as an opportunity. You probably figured Guvelly would get a warrant and search my shop for the stolen pot. In order to beat him to the punch, you came into my shop using the key I gave you and searched for the pot."

"You are out of your mind," he said.

"You brought a screwdriver and took the hinges off my storage cabinets. When you didn't find the pot, you put the hinges back to cover your tracks. But you left your fingerprints on them."

He gave me a big, mean smile. "That's impossible."

Four more words. That's what I was hoping for. Just four more words. And when he said, "That's impossible," I thought for sure those four words were about to come out of his mouth: "I wiped them off."

But he didn't fall for it. I've seen things like that work in movies, but maybe real life is different. But I had a backup plan.

"It doesn't matter. You are in here quite frequently, so having your prints in my shop wouldn't be enough to convict you of anything."

"Damn right," he said.

"But why would you be in here at 6:57 in the morning?"

No one spoke up, so I answered my own question. "I had a laser beam across my front door that registered the time that anyone passed over the threshold. On the morning after Guvelly first came to see me, someone crossed that beam at 6:57 AM. My nephew, Tristan, installed the device and read the log. He informed me that someone had crossed my threshold at 6:57 and that the next signal break was recorded at 9:22 that same morning. I originally thought that 9:22 break was you coming to see me, Reg. But I later remembered an airplane pilot telling me the most important thing about flying was that the number of landings and takeoffs should always be equal. In a shop, the number of comings and goings must also be equal. There was nothing between 6:57 and 9:22. So, whomever came in at 6:57 had to go out at 9:22. And that was you, Reggie."

"I'm sorry for you, my friend," said Reggie, "you seem somewhat confused."

"Maybe you're right." I paused for a few seconds then asked, "Who do *you* think killed Guvelly?"

The smile he gave me was poisonous. "Maybe you did. After all, the body was found in your shop."

Yes! I thought to myself with jubilation. Sometimes these tricks do work. Sometimes the bad guys do hang themselves.

"How do you know where the body was found?" asked Fletcher.

Reggie's eyes clouded as he thought about what he had said. "I read it in the paper," he tried.

"It wasn't in the paper," said Whit.

We all sat there in silence while Reggie considered his options. Finally he turned to me. "You're a sniveling little wimp, Schuze. While I was off defending this country, you were living the good life as a student. You're a lazy, undisciplined weakling living off pots you dig up because you're too lazy to do any honest work."

The cops had moved around him, but he continued his trade. "I tried to help you, man. But what do I get? Treachery. Well, listen up, wimp. You may have the upper hand now, but I'm coming after you, man, and I'll grind you in the dirt like a worm."

I have to tell you, I was scared even though the uniformed policemen had cuffed him.

63

"Wow, Uncle Hubert. You were like Sherlock Holmes tonight."

Tristan was eating the dip made from the onion soup mix and enjoying a beer from my fridge.

"Sherlock Holmes," I said, "lived in rented rooms and took drugs."

"Whatever. And on top of that, you're a local hero. I can't believe it. My uncle is in the newspaper as a murder suspect and a pot thief, and all my friends are calling me to say how cool it is that you're my uncle."

I shrugged.

"But you didn't kill anyone, and you didn't really steal anything, did you?"

"Well," I said, "I certainly didn't murder anyone. As far as the theft issue, that sort of depends on your definition of—"

"I knew it. And you recovered the pot that was stolen from the Museum, and they made a lot of money at the auction to help students."

"That's true," I admitted.

"What's that music?"

"Billie Holiday."

"I like it."

"You never told me about the girl you took to that alternative to music concert."

"Alternative music, not alternative *to* music."

"Right."

"Selena. I'm not seeing her anymore."

I dipped a chip into the pecan and peaches dip. Miss Gladys was right. It was better than it sounds. Then I decided I had to have a beer.

Tristan said, "Aren't you going to ask me why?"

"I didn't want to pry."

"It's not prying. I like having you to talk to about these things."

"This isn't going to be a birds and bees discussion, is it?"

He laughed that deep laugh that seems to come up from his stomach and has a tremolo to it. "I hope not."

"Whew," I replied.

"She just came on too strong. I was cool with her asking me to go to the concert. I don't think guys always have to do the asking. But all night long she kept asking me questions about myself, and she didn't pay much attention to the music. She's really good looking, and I think she's smart, but . . ." His voice trailed off.

"Did you see her again after the concert?"

"Yeah. I decided it was my turn, so I took her to a movie. Afterwards we went for coffee, and while I was trying to talk about the movie, she was talking about herself—what she likes and doesn't like and all, and the same things about me—what do I like, what do I not like. I guess that's normal. When you date someone, you want to get to know each other."

"Tristan, getting to know someone isn't a matter of cataloging what they like and don't like. You don't tell people who you are. You show them. Dates are opportunities to do things—hear music, see movies, go rafting. You get a feel for someone by seeing them do things and doing those things with them. It's okay to ask questions, of course. But when it comes to 'show and tell,' dating is more about showing than telling."

"Wow, Uncle Hubert. I guess wisdom does come with age. You really put your finger on it. I wanted to do things with her, but she just wanted to interview me."

"Well, I'm pushing middle age and still live alone in the back of a shop, so I don't think I qualify as an expert on relationships. Who are you seeing now?"

He took out his i-thingy and pretended to scroll through a long list.

"I think I've run out of memory," he said.

"I can see that not hitting it off with Selena has you really broken up."

He laughed. "Thanks for the talk. And thanks for including me tonight. It was a radically new experience for me. And it's also good to see bad guys get caught."

"Yes, and as you said, the University got a scholarship out of the deal."

"But the scholarship is limited to art students. That's a real bummer. I mean art scholarships are so easy to get. Everybody wants to help the starving artists. But does anyone ever stop to think why they're starving? It's because they're not providing a good or service people really need. I mean, there's an artist on every street corner. But everyone needs help with their computer, don't they? There are millions of people like you, Uncle Hubert, who don't know the first things about computers—no disrespect intended—and they could use the help of a college graduate professional. But do we have enough of them? No. And why? Because there's not enough scholarship money for computer majors. It all goes to art students. And on top of that—"

"Tristan?"

"Yes?"

"How much do you need?"

64

I guess I don't have to tell you where Susannah and I were the next night.

"That was some confrontation last night," she said.

"I'm just glad the cops were out in force. I think Reggie would have killed me with his bare hands."

"Which reminds me. I have some questions. You told me Tristan speculated that the person who came into your shop at 6:57 must have stepped over the beam when he left. That could still be true, couldn't it?"

"Not really. If that had happened, there would have to be *two* later interruptions that morning, one when Reggie came in and one when he left. But there was only one, the one at 9:22."

"Okay. But when Reggie searched your place and didn't find the Bandelier pot, why didn't he just take some of the other stuff? After all, you have a lot of valuable pots."

"True. But like Hugo Berdal, he wouldn't know how to fence

them. And he probably didn't want to risk it. But if he could find the pot Guvelly had described to him, he knew he could get the finder's fee."

"But when he didn't find that pot, why kill Guvelly?"

"I'm not sure. My guess is that Guvelly and his colleagues had me under surveillance. Maybe they saw Reggie sneak into my place in the middle of the night and thought he was involved somehow. Guvelly confronted him. They argued. Reggie has quite a temper."

"Do you think we'll ever know?"

I shrugged. "Maybe Reggie will tell all to get a better sentencing deal."

"Why did the two firstNAtions goons come to threaten you?"

"Crow and Smith had the cooperation of Guvelly to run their protection racket. So he could order them to scare me in the hope that I would crack and give them the pot."

"But you didn't have the pot."

"Yeah, but they didn't know that."

"What will happen to them?"

"Nothing. Crow and Smith were granted immunity in exchange for testifying that they saw Nordquist and Berdal arrive together at the Hyatt. They also agreed, as part of the deal, to end their protection racket."

"You think they will?"

"No, but they'll probably move it somewhere else."

We waved to Angie for more salsa and chips.

"You must be feeling pretty good right now," Susannah said to me.

"I do. The pots are back where they belong, the bad guys are in jail, and Kaylee and Arturo have found true happiness."

"But Consuela is no better."

"It's real life, Suze. Not everything gets resolved. But she and Emilio seem as happy now as they were before she got sick. Maybe true love does conquer all."

"I still believe that," she said. Her eyes were moist but there was a smile on her face.

"I have something for you," she said and handed me a cardboard tube.

I removed the end cap, extracted a piece of paper, unrolled it and saw a fascinating drawing. Two thin lines captured the look of a desert horizon. Two vertical stylized arms met at that horizon, and their hands wound around each other like a double helix. The double helix formed a pot. The entire thing hinted at the Zia sun, New Mexico's symbol. The lines were simple yet highly suggestive of the Southwest.

I looked up at Susannah. "This is great work. Did you draw this?"

"No. My friends drew it. That's your new logo."

I had forgotten all about the logo project. "It's fantastic."

"You really like it?"

"More than I can say."

"So you'll use it for your business?"

"Absolutely."

"Well," she said, "now that you've seen the logo, does any name for your shop leap to mind."

I looked at the hand coming up from the soil and thought of the spirits of the ancient potters.

"Spirits in Clay," I announced.

"That's a great name. I'll tell my friends about it."

I hesitated a few seconds then asked, "Feeling better today?"

"Not much. But at least I've stopped crying every five minutes. Are my eyes still bloodshot?"

"They are, but the swelling in your nose seems to have gone down."

"Thanks a lot." She slumped back in her chair and looked at me. "You think either one of us will ever find that certain someone?"

"You will, Suze. I'm certain of it. As for me, well, Kaylee may have been my last shot."

She laughed and choked briefly then laughed again.

"I've got something here I think you'll like," I said.

I handed her a section of the *Los Angeles Times*. I had circled the article with the headline that read *Local Professor Arrested for Art Theft*.

As she read she kept glancing up at me and her look evolved from incredulous to pleased. "I can't believe this. The only time that bastard was ever in the Valle del Rio was when I gave him a private tour after his lecture. And while I was being such a great host and fawning student, he was stealing a Remington right under my nose."

"Maybe not," I said. "Read the related story right below."

"Art Historian's Troubles Inflate," she read aloud. The story read, "Kauffmann Williburton, the well-known art historian accused of stealing a Remington bronze from a museum in New Mexico, is experiencing troubles on another front as well. The police search of his house turned up not only the missing Remington under the couch in the living room but also an inflatable woman under the bed in the master bedroom. The police took no action since possession of an inflatable woman is not illegal in California, but Mrs. Williburton is suing for divorce."

"Hubie! That's Berdal's woman."

I just smiled.

"And you took the Remington when you were switching pots with Doak."

Another smile. But nothing to match Susannah's. Then she started laughing, and I started laughing with her. And we both kept laughing as we waved for Angie.

Acknowledgments

I owe much to my agents, Barbara Bitela and Ed Silver of the Silver Bitela Agency and Philip Turner of Philip Turner Book Productions. Ed, Babz and Philip have improved my books, found me publishers and encouraged me along the way.

Thanks to Roger Paulding for his editing.

I also want to thank my daughter, Claire, who—although a scholar—willingly serves as alpha reader for my pulp fiction.

About the Author

J. Michael Orenduff grew up in a house so close to the Rio Grande that he could Frisbee a tortilla into Mexico from his backyard. While studying for an MA at the University of New Mexico, he worked during the summer as a volunteer teacher at one of the nearby pueblos. After receiving a PhD from Tulane University, he became a professor. He went on to serve as president of New Mexico State University.

Orenduff took early retirement from higher education to write his award-winning Pot Thief murder mysteries, which combine archaeology and philosophy with humor and mystery. Among the author's many accolades are the Lefty Award for best humorous mystery, the Epic Award for best mystery or suspense ebook, and the New Mexico Book Award for best mystery or suspense fiction. His books have been described by the *Baltimore Sun* as "funny at a very high intellectual level" and "deliciously delightful," and by the *El Paso Times* as "the perfect fusion of murder, mayhem and margaritas."

THE POT THIEF MYSTERIES

FROM OPEN ROAD MEDIA

Available wherever ebooks are sold

Made in the USA
Lexington, KY
20 February 2015